DUKE

(LONDON BOYS II)

REBECCA CASTLE

ISBN: 9780645395983

To my friends in London.
Thank you all for the best ten years.
Cheerio.

"Murder, I have often noticed, is a great matchmaker."

AGATHA CHRISTIE

PROLOGUE

GRACE

"The murderer is targeting *King*?"

I sit there as I ask the crazy question, staring at my flat-mate in complete disbelief at how everything in our world has completely changed in the last couple of minutes.

A murderer is after her boyfriend. She's just told me, and now I am in shock.

What the actual fuck?

It was only a few moments ago when King, Scarlett, and I were sitting around the kitchen table eating breakfast and laughing. Morning banter. All so totally innocent.

I was sitting there feeling so happy for my flatmate as she flirted and lovingly touched her new boyfriend. She's had a really rough time the last few weeks, but now she has finally found a man who clearly loves her for *her*. Seeing your best friend elated like that can only make you feel on top of the world.

And then it all comes crashing down. In a matter of seconds.

The gorgeous son of a billionaire got a text message from his brother saying the same murderer who'd killed his publicist a few weeks ago has just now handed in a note to the police stating his intent to kill King.

And we all know this has ruined everything we just had moments ago in a heartbeat.

King immediately rushed out the door, leaving his girlfriend and me alone to recover from the sudden news. It's like whiplash has hit us. I sit there and Scarlett stands. Completely still. Neither of us can believe it.

Scarlett's boyfriend shrugged the threat off in front of us like it was nothing. He's a tall, imposing guy and wants to project that to everyone around him, including his girlfriend. Six-foot something with a body that's *mightily* fine. He has to play the confident alpha, but I knew something was up the second his eyes scanned the message. His bravado was all clearly an act to make his girlfriend feel calm. But Scarlett and I aren't stupid. We see straight through it.

We know this is deadly serious.

Someone is out for Kingsley's blood.

Bloody hell.

"This is crazy," I say to my flatmate once her boyfriend leaves. "Why would someone go after him like this? Go after him acting like some comic book villain with all these threats? Do you know why?"

Scarlett shakes her head. She's in as much shock as I am.

Everything was going so well for her this morning that to be faced with this awful news is just simply heartbreaking. Kingsley had, just last evening, romantically professed his love to her at the bar of the tallest building in London before spending the night here. Having lots of fun in Scarlett's bedroom, I bet. If I wasn't so world-weary, then I would say it sounded like they were enthusiastically jumping on her bed all night long.

Scarlett has really needed a break and not have a murderer showing up at her door. She's new to London. An American who traveled all the way here across the Pond to live out her dreams of working in theater and seeing the history and culture of Europe. She couldn't find a place to live nor a place to work until she luckily met me. We found each other at a time when we both needed a friend, and now we've become the best of friends. She ended up renting my spare room and then got a job working at the Prestige Theater.

And that's where she met Kingsley.

Again.

The famous actor who disappeared from her life was on stage at the theater she worked at.

He'd spent a week at Scarlett's high school back in America years ago, and then he broke her teenage heart by moving back here.

But then they rediscovered each other in the most unlikely of circumstances.

And now they're in love.

My little heart can't take the cuteness.

But all of that has been halted by some asshole who's murdered King's publicist on the theater's stage.

"I guess they must be after him because of his family name," Scarlett replies to me once King leaves.

I stare back at her blankly. She had introduced Kingsley to me before, but she's never told me his last name. I have no inkling why his family would be involved in all this.

What does she even mean? What kind of family name is powerful enough to make someone threaten to kill you?

"Who?" I ask. "What family?"

"His family is some rich noble name that goes back so

many generations," Scarlett says. "Have you heard of them? Heath-Harding."

And that's when my whole world stops.

That name.

That fucking name.

I gasp when it rolls out of Scarlett's mouth. She has no clue - *absolutely no idea at all* - what that name means to me. How it echoes through my past.

"I should've guessed," I whisper, my voice trembling. "I should've seen it the moment you introduced me to Kingsley. I should've put two and two together. He even *looks* like him, for goodness' sake."

"Who?" Scarlett asks, confused.

"*Kingsley* Heath-Harding. Of course. It's such an unusual name. It should've rung alarm bells from the moment I saw him."

"What are you saying, Grace? I don't understand you."

So many emotions bubble through me as I slowly come to terms with what she's just told me. It's bigger news than the fact the killer is now after King.

It's insane how one simple double-barreled posh name can affect me, but it does. I am shaken to my core.

And then I decide to tell her.

"I know his brother," I say quietly. "Duke Heath-Harding."

"What? You know Duke? You're friends?"

"I know him more than just *friends*," I reply, smiling. "We had a thing. Years ago."

"A thing?"

"We kinda dated," I say, almost blushing at the memory. "A long time ago. He's the boy who got away. The boy who broke my heart."

Duke Heath-Harding.

I cannot believe it.

Bloody, bloody hell.

Of course he's King's brother. I really should've seen it.

His name is like an apparition. Like when you listen to a song that takes you back years to the place you first heard it, when all the sights and sounds flood back into your memory so that it feels so *real.* Like you're experiencing it again as if it's the first time. That's who Duke Heath-Harding is for me. He's my song that I haven't heard for a very long time.

"Wow. Everything is happening at once," Scarlett says, sitting back down in the chair. "You need to tell me every single detail."

I will tell her.

I'll tell her everything I've been trying to hide from for four years.

Now that she and King are together, then that means one thing for me. It is now a certainty that my path will soon cross with Duke's again.

Jesus. I will really see him again, won't I?

And this time I better prepare my heart, because I can't have it hurt as much as it did last time I saw that gorgeous man.

How he and I first met? How did he break my heart? Why I'm so absolutely terrified of seeing him again?

Well, let me tell you...

1

FOUR YEARS EARLIER

GRACE

IT ALL STARTS four years ago.

It was my first day working at Small - a quirky interior design shop located in the heart of Notting Hill in West London - when I first met Duke Heath-Harding.

And like all first days at a new place, I was nervous as hell.

I was eighteen, and this was my first ever job, so I was not only just nervous, but I was also practically *peeing* my pants in sheer bloody terror.

It took me walking around the block three times, hyping myself up by listening to some pretty intense rock songs on my headphones, before I summoned up the courage to go in.

The bell rang on the latch as I stepped into Small, not knowing what awaited me.

"Hello," a middle-aged woman wearing very large and thick glasses and big, frizzy hair greeted me from behind the counter. "How may I help?"

"I'm looking for Mabel," I squeaked out extra nervously in my hesitant teenager voice. "My name's Grace. I'm starting work here today."

The woman's penetrating gaze traveled up from my legs, over my fidgeting hands, and to my black shoulder-length hair as if she was inspecting a piece of rotten meat. I clearly did not live up to whatever standards she was judging me by.

Oh God, it's going bad already and I'm not even two steps inside.

"Hm," the woman started. Her evaluation was clearly not positive. "I'm Mabel. You and I spoke over email, didn't we?"

"Yes. It's nice to meet you," I replied, offering out my hand with a cheerful smile. She shook it limply, as if I was wasting her precious time.

"Can you handle money?" she asked me.

Straight in with the questions? Okay. You can do this, Grace.

"Well, I do spend a lot of money," I replied. "On clothes. I'm pretty impulsive. So, yeah, I have handled a lot of cash, but it's usually leaving my hands."

I try a little laugh, but her dour expression did not change.

"Okay, then. Follow me around today and watch what I do. Watch *exactly* what I do. I expect not to show you things twice, you understand?"

"Crystal clear."

Mabel winced. It was like every word that came out of my mouth made her cringe.

"Get yourself orientated with Small. Treat

8

everything *carefully*. This is my shop that I've owned for twenty years, and it is to be run exactly to my liking. Not one thing out of place. I have not maintained an impeccable reputation with the lovely people of Notting Hill for nothing."

"I got you."

"I've had the most amazing customers through these doors," Mabel continued in a brisk and stern tone, as if she were talking to a child. "I am well known in this community. I've had movie stars, politicians, Lords and Ladies call me up personally to design their homes. I will not let it all fall apart because some rowdy *teenager* can't add up to ten, you understand?"

I nod. Anxiety gripped me even tighter than before I entered the shop. This woman was so intimidating. I was coming to realize there was not a single speck of humor in her. "I do."

She then proceeded to show me around the store whilst rattling off an impressive list of famous people's names who she'd met. There had been quite a few celebs who've shopped in Small, and Mabel did not lose an opportunity to tell me about every single one who'd breezed through her doors.

The name of the store perfectly fitted its size. There was not enough space to spin around in, especially when it was all cluttered up by what Small sold.

It's hard to describe what exactly was the kind of shop Small was. Everything seemed to be completely random. Fancy items for fancy houses would be the best way to pin the shop's displays down. Things that, I guess, rich people decorate their homes with in order to make other people think they have a personality. Some artworks. Some cool tribal things that were supposedly from Africa. Wind instruments that didn't really work. Lights that couldn't light up a room but were sculptured to look very pretty. That kind of junk that the rich bourgeois denizens of Notting Hill would just eat up.

"This is cool," I said, pointing at a long wooden tube with exquisite painting dotting around the outside that was displayed in one corner.

"That's a Didgeridoo," Mabel replied like I'm stupid. "They're a traditional Indigenous Australian instrument, but this one doesn't make any sound."

"Oh, right."

Mabel took a moment to look me up and down, as if noticing me for the first time again.

"If you are going to work here, then you better dress better than you've done today," she said, making a face at my clothes. "Something not like this."

She gestured a manicured finger towards me.

What?

I glanced down at my dark jeans and shirt. I was sure that morning they were appropriate clothes for being a shop assistant. Plain. Smart casual.

"Is something wrong with how I look?" I asked, hurt.

I didn't think I was going to be judged this much today...

"Just dress... *nicer*," Mabel replied coldly.

I gulped.

She really thinks I'm trash, doesn't she?

"Um, okay."

Mabel continued to name-drop more famous people as she took me into the back of the store to show me the office and stockroom, seemingly to completely forget that she had just ripped my ego and dress sense to shreds. It seemed like Mabel knew every celebrity in Britain. At least her incessant boasting was taking the edge off my nerves.

That was, until she aimed her fire back on me.

"Do you go to any dinner parties?" she asked me.

I blinked. Confused. I had completely drifted off and had not paid any attention to what Mabel had said for the last few minutes. I thought she was still listing off names.

"Uh. No," I stammered. "I haven't really been to any dinner parties."

She scoffed and eyed me condescendingly from under her thick glasses and frizzy hair.

"It's a very *civilized* thing to do," she said. "Dinner parties are my favorite social event. If you know the right people, as I do, then you can go to the best ones. I've met a lot of my customers at Notting Hill dinner parties, but don't let that intimidate you. I'm quite a well-beloved local figure."

I nodded along. I didn't really care how much the woman wanted to name-drop; I just needed a job. I didn't really care for celebrities or fame; I was just happy to be in a shop earning money.

"How many other staff members work here?" I asked her.

"Just you and me," Mabel replies seriously. "*If* you behave yourself and don't mess up, that is. You'll do for now."

Great. I'll do. For now.

For the next few hours, I settled into my new job. It was a bit weird at first, with Mabel hovering over my shoulder like a bad smell, constantly checking up on me and everything I was doing like a hawk. Maybe she suspected that I would attempt to steal money from her till. She needn't have worried. I could barely operate the old thing.

It seemed like Mabel had refused to move on since the sixties. Everything in the store was old-fashioned technology. There was not a computer in sight. It might've added to the cool antique vibe of the place, but it made things ten times more difficult for me.

Look, I'm a Millennial kid. I've grown up on smartphones and laptops, not typewriters and Walkmans. How Mabel operated was like another world to me.

Sweat poured off me as I tried to work out customers' orders on the analog devices, whilst Mabel kept a beady eye on every movement of mine. It was exhausting and pretty disheartening, but I tried. I *really* did try. I wanted to make this job work. I really needed the money.

At one point, Mabel went into the office at the back of the shop, telling me she was making a phone call. I was left alone to fend for myself. Luckily, there were no customers in the place, so I decided to have another look around the place. I found myself drawn to the Didgeridoo my new boss had shown me. She had said it didn't work, but I was tempted to give it a try.

I puckered my lips over the opening and blew.

And no sound came out.

Oh.

Mabel was right.

I quickly darted back around to the back of the counter, feeling like a naughty schoolgirl. Mabel appeared, not having the slightest clue at what I'd been up to. She took her place behind me, observing me like a hawk yet again.

The front doorbell rang, and another customer stepped in. Back to work.

And then, a few hours later as evening descended on London, the shop cleared and Mabel tapped my shoulder.

"Right. I'm off now," she said. "I'm going to a dinner party with a group of some very famous people. I can't tell you their names, obviously, but they're very well known. You'd recognize them."

"Oh, okay."

Something about the way she said that made me think she was definitely not going to a dinner party with a bunch of famous people and that, in all likelihood, she was just heading home to drink a bottle of wine alone. Call it a hunch.

"So, I will leave you to close up the store," Mabel told me. "I trust you do it correctly."

She passed by the counter and opened the front door. The bell rung.

"What..."

I started to ask her how to even close up, as I had *zero* clue on how to do it, but Mabel wouldn't hear a word of it. She interrupted me with her sharp bark.

"Make sure you lock up properly. I will be checking in the morning. Here are the keys."

From across the shop, she threw them at me. Like I was her slave.

I barely caught them before they could clatter to the floor and when I looked up, Mabel was gone.

I was alone. To do something I didn't even know how to do.

Oh no. Flipping heck.

My sweating returned with a force as I fumbled around with the front door lock. I thought I had managed it. I tried pulling the door, and it didn't budge at all. So. Yeah. It worked.

I hoped.

I guessed the next step was to clear the clutter from around the till. I wanted to give a good impression to Mabel when she opened in the morning. For her to think I was not a totally useless mess. Feeling like I was taking the initiative, I started to pack receipts and loose papers into boxes to place under the counter, bending over to make sure everything was pushed into place. My jeans slid down a few inches, and I felt my ass crack expose itself to the elements.

And that's when the bell on the front door rang.

Shit.

Someone had entered the shop. The door had not been locked properly.

And my ass was in the air, pointed directly right at them.

My ass crack perfectly in view.

2

GRACE

Oh, crap. Oh, crap. Oh, crap.

The moment I heard the front doorbell ring, I tried to stand up as fast as I could in a desperate attempt to try to not to give the customer a full-on view of my bum perked up in the air.

But it was too late for that. I knew they'd seen it all. Probably a whole load of my lovely ass crack as well.

Oh crap indeed.

I started to blabber.

"Sorry, we're actually..."

I didn't even get the chance to finish my sentence and tell the customer to leave when I looked up and I locked eyes with them.

Locked eyes with *him.*

Holy shit, this man is beautiful.

The first thing I noticed was his own eyes. They were a deep blue that pierced straight through me as he stood there in the store's doorway. Glowing at me from under short jet-black hair that was fashioned into some irresistible curls. His full lips were formed into a slight smile. I assumed he was amused from seeing my embarrassing ass. And his jawline was impeccable. There was literally nothing wrong with this guy.

His body practically yelled confidence and dominance. *Fuck. Me.*

He was exactly the kind of man I didn't want to have just seen me in such a compromising position, bending over.

He was tall, at least six feet. Plus a few inches. His broad shoulders dominated the front door as he entered. His muscles were defined even through the nice suit he was wearing.

My words turned to jelly in my mouth and my sentence trailed off. My knees shook under me when I realized that I had just displayed my fat ass to this gorgeous man, but that still didn't stop heat to surge between my legs from just looking at this guy.

What a man. What a specimen.

My first thought was to praise the Lord.

Thank you, God, for creating such art. You did good with this one. Well done, big guy.

I instantly felt a connection with this man. Or perhaps it was just my hormones firing off by being presented with a man worthy enough to wrap my legs around. Whatever it was, my entire demeanor changed, and I instantly became like a little schoolgirl feeling like I had just been caught doing something naughty.

"Oh, I'm so sorry, sir. We are supposed to be closed, so I was just picking up some things here behind the counter and I didn't expect anyone to come in and then you did, and then I guess you saw my ass in the air. Oh my God, I am so sorry you had to see that. I thought the door was locked, but clearly it wasn't. It's only my first day."

Wow. I can really gobble on like a turkey when I want to.

What a shitshow.

The gorgeous man just stood there with a small smile on his face, casually observing the embarrassing string of words I was rambling at him with. I closed my mouth shut, willing myself with all the force in my body to stop talking. To stop before I could humiliate myself further.

You've done plenty, Grace, you nitwit.

"You're funny," the man said in a deep, sexy voice. My legs buckled under me at his sound. I gripped the counter like a lifeboat to steady myself. I had never seen or heard, a man so goddamn perfect in every way.

"Well, I'd prefer funny to being embarrassing. Which I definitely just was and which you definitely just saw."

"You have nothing to be ashamed of," he replied calmly. "We've all been there."

Hm. Something told me that this guy had probably never been in an embarrassing situation in his life, and certainly not one where he showed his ass crack to a complete stranger. How could he have been when he looked like *that*?

"It seems like I land myself in something stupid every second day, but cheers. Thanks for trying to make me feel better about myself. You're a very kind man."

Kind man? Just shut up, Grace. You're talking way too much.

"Is it alright if I browse for a moment?" the guy asked, his eyes flickering over the inside of the store and all the wacky items on the shelves. "I know you just said that you're closed, but I would love to have a quick look around. It'll be only for a few minutes, and I won't get in your way. I promise."

I mean. *Jesus.* The man could take as long as he wanted. I wasn't complaining in the slightest.

"Uh, yeah. Sure."

I nodded along like a daft bimbo, trying really hard not to seem like I wanted to have this man's babies.

I was obviously failing.

I pretended to scan through some pages as he walked around the tiny shop. Under the counter, I tried to adjust my jeans so that my lovely ass crack could no longer be seen. I made all the required rustling of papers to make it appear that I was totally immersed in anything other than this six-foot hunk just casually strolling around only a few inches away from me. He remained firmly within my peripheral vision.

"Do you need any help?" I eventually asked him once I had run out of things to fidget around with. "Searching for anything in particular?"

The man shook his head. "No, I'm fine. Just having a quick look, thanks."

I watched him walk over to the same Didgeridoo instrument that Mabel had shown me earlier. He observed it carefully, curious.

"That one doesn't work," I said, nodding at the long wooden tube. "I secretly tried it earlier when my boss wasn't looking, and nothing came out."

The man frowned. "I was fortunate enough to spend a few months in Australia when I was a teenager assisting in building a school for Indigenous kids," he replied. "I've luckily played a few Didgeridoos in my time. I'll give this one a try if that's okay with you?"

"By all means, but I honestly don't think it'll do anything, no matter how hard you blow."

"Well, if it doesn't make a sound, then I'll be as embarrassed as you, won't I?"

He pulled the tip of it towards his mouth and blew.

To my shock, the instrument made a gorgeous resonating sound. The man kept blowing, and therefore sustained the noise as it reverberated around the room. The sound was positively otherworldly. I'd felt like I'd been transported to the deep Australian bush.

"Wow," I remarked when he removed his mouth from the opening. The man smiled at me.

I wonder what else he can do well with his mouth...

"*Now* you have to be embarrassed," he said. "Saying something as beautiful as this doesn't work? What a travesty."

I blushed. "I am definitely embarrassed, trust me."

"Pretty pathetic shopkeeping skills, to be honest. First, you show me your ass and then you tell me something perfectly fine doesn't work. Your first day isn't going so well, isn't it?"

"It most certainly is not."

"Let me be the proper judge of that. How has the rest of your day been?"

"You want to hear about my terrible first day?"

He shrugged. "Honey, I've got time."

"Well, my manager has left me all alone to close up."

"On your first day?"

"Yep."

"Wow."

"And I've just been completely stressed about every-thing," I said. I didn't know why I was telling this man all my secrets. He was just so easy to talk to. And he listened. His blue eyes stared back at me, completely transfixed by every stupid word I uttered. I didn't know why he was looking at me like that. "I feel like I've done every possible thing wrong. I must look like a total mess."

The man placed down the instrument and walked

purposely towards me. My breath caught in my throat as he stared me down. He stopped just inches away from my breasts. I felt my nipples harden at the sight of him standing so close.

He smelled of both amber and citrus. Like wild nature. Freedom. I wanted to breathe him in, but I couldn't even work my lungs when he was so near.

"You're not a mess," he said softly.

He did not blink his hard blue eyes as he reached forward with his hand and took my chin between two fingers, lifting my blushing face up to meet his directly.

My body's insides were on fire as his stare burned into me.

He then whispered two words that rocked my core.

Two words that summed up the sheer confidence and *presence* of this man.

"You're pretty."

3

GRACE

THOSE TWO WORDS of his hit me like a tidal wave.

You're pretty.

Like, damn. This boy was smooth as ice. He knew *exactly* how to make me go all gooey inside with just a whisper.

Blimey.

I'd never been called pretty by a guy before, especially not one who was built like that. With that kind of jawline. It makes me all jittery, and I'm usually the type of girl to present a steely front to the world. I've experienced my fair share of hardship to be undone by a strange man. But there I was. That was happening to me. That man was unraveling me like a loose bow in the middle of that store.

And I was willingly submitting to his sway.

I had no words for him. I just blinked up into his piercing blue eyes. The man was unfazed by my silence.

"How about you show me around?" he asked me.

My mouth went dry.

"Sure," I replied.

He smiled. "Great."

His fingers let go of my chin and he took a step back. I let out an involuntary sigh as he did so. All the tension flooded out of my body and feeling returned to my limbs.

It's like he just cast a spell over me...

"Are you planning on buying anything specific?" I asked him, my voice returning.

The man - whose name I did not even know yet - shrugged. "I'll see what I like the look of. I'll know what I want when I see it."

"You're that kind of man? Decisive?"

"Very much so. I always know what I want."

But he was not looking at anything in the store. The only thing he was focused on was me.

Oh God, he wanted *me*.

No. You're just imagining that, Grace. Calm down. You're a tough girl. You can't fall over head-over-heels with a man you don't even know the name of yet.

But I was falling hopelessly head-over-heels with a total stranger. And I was so hoping I was that specific thing he liked the look of.

"Well, we have a lot of different things you can decorate your home with," I said, gesturing towards a corner of the store. "Even a whole range of cutlery for your kitchen. A lot of this stuff is handcrafted."

I had to get his overpowering attention away from my body. I didn't think I could handle any more of his intensity.

"Where's the handcrafted stuff?" he asked quietly.

"Just here."

The man followed my hand to a shelf full of various plates and kitchen utensils. He browsed through the range, stopping at one old-fashioned white bowl.

"Funny," he chuckled softly.

"What is it?"

He pointed to the inside of the bowl. "That's my name right there."

I peered over his broad shoulder to read what he was indicating at. There was a name painted in the bottom of the bowl in cursive writing.

Duke.

It must've been some decorative thing the maker of the bowl had done. Something to sound fancy. Make it easier to sell to people readily impressed with fancy names, I guessed. To be honest, I had no clue. I was a pretty pathetic salesgirl.

I sniggered. "Your name's Duke?"

The man's face remained serious. "What's wrong with it?"

"*Duke*?"

"Yes, it is. That's my name."

"No way."

"It's true," he replied stonily. "What's wrong with it?"

I realized he really was being serious.

"Oh. I'm sorry. I've just never met a Duke before."

"Well, now you have."

If he was insulted by my laughter, he didn't show it. It seemed like nothing could shake this man. His whole demeanor oozed an unbreakable self-confidence.

"Nice to meet you, Duke," I said. "I'm Grace. A more normal name."

"My name's normal."

"Come on, no one is called Duke."

"You might be true there," he replied with a wink. "But it does make me unique. Would you agree?"

Oh, I certainly do.

"You're unique, that's for sure," I replied. I tried to keep my eyes up on Duke's and not down on his perfect body in that nice suit. "So, what's your last name, mister Duke?"

"Duke Heath-Harding."

Bloody hell. He's like a knight from a fairy tale.

"That's your full name?"

He smiled. "There are some middle ones I won't bore you with."

"You have *more* names?"

"Yep, a whole bunch of middle names are in there somewhere."

"Sounds posh."

"That's because it is," Duke replied.

"Oh."

He's stating the obvious, Grace, and it still went over your head.

"You could say I'm pretty posh," he continued.

"Right."

Wow. The man must be loaded. Double-barreled with that kind of cut-glass accent meant one thing. Nobility. He was probably descended from some aristocratic family. That was so far removed from who I was. From my commoner heritage.

It made him even more mysterious.

He probably had a lot of money. He was probably super educated. Just from the way he carried himself certainly marked him out as *elite*.

But why would he tell me his full name? I was sure a sophisticated guy like him wouldn't say anything without thinking. He must've known I would go home and search him up immediately upon him leaving the store. That'd be the only reason why he would divulge his entire name, right?

Right?

I mean, why else would he drop it into our conversation like that?

"So, is my name a cool one?" he asked me. "Does it live up to Grace's standard?"

I giggled. "Maybe. A little."

"And what would I have to do to reach your lofty standards, Grace?"

"I dunno," I mumbled.

God. I was terrible at flirting.

But you can't blame me. How can any girl hold her nerve with a man like that standing in front of them, directing his entire focus on you? Definitely not me, and it was really showing.

Duke smiled again - *God, that smile* - and then placed the plate with his name back on the shelf.

"Well, thank you, Grace, for showing me around. Maybe one day I will meet your high standards."

And then he turned and headed towards the exit, giving me a sexy wink before he pushed the unlocked door.

I whimpered a feeble goodbye before he was out onto the street.

I watched, completely still, as he rounded a corner and disappeared from view. He was gone.

"What the fuck just happened?" I asked myself in the silence of his exit.

His words still echoed, unchecked, around my head.

You're pretty.

Oh, I was definitely going to find out more about Duke Heath-Harding.

4

GRACE

OF COURSE, I googled Duke Heath-Harding. I did it the moment I jumped onto the bus on the long way across London, back to my flat. The same flat my mother once owned, and who passed it onto me in her will.

My mom had died a year before I started the job at Small. Her passing was a horrific last few months to experience. All hospital white walls and gray waiting rooms. Tubes and nurses. I'd spent a year picking up the pieces of my shattered life after she'd gone. Trying to get back on track even though I was only eighteen and had just become my own woman. It was not the best start to adulthood, but I had managed to force myself through the grief and now had finally got a job. I had spent a year losing myself in true crime documentaries and fiction books to ease the pain. A year trying to get over the loss of my best friend.

I dreamed of living a better life. Of being treated like a princess. And now I had finally dragged myself out of the flat I had once shared with my mother to face life. To face the big bad world.

And then Duke Heath-Harding dropped into that store on my first day like a thunderbolt, and I simply just had to find out everything about this mysterious man who had just witnessed my ass bouncing in the air.

It was not hard to find his name. There were so many articles about the Heath-Harding family online. I clicked on the top article that popped up. It was some puff piece about the two sons of Lord Heath-Harding. Duke and Kingsley. I read through it greedily.

The family was exactly what I expected them to be. Billionaire aristocrats with generations of history under their name. They seemingly owned half of England. The two brothers were the toast of the London social scene. Two drop-dead gorgeous bachelors with names that could open doors and endless pockets full of money.

No way was Duke Heath-Harding actually interested in me. It was obvious I was just a little fun plaything for this billionaire to flirt with for a while in a shop as he browsed, nothing more.

But still, sitting on that bus as it trundled eternally through the dark evening streets of London, I continued to dive deeper into who he was.

A girl can have a moment of fantasy, can't she?

There was not much about his personal history. Despite the famous family name, it seemed like Duke kept to himself. Well, as private as a sought-after bachelor could be.

But his privacy was no match for my detective skills. After all, I had just spent a year amongst inspectors and the most successful serial killers of all time through my television screen. I could hunt down some billionaire bad boy any day of the week. Easy.

And I did. On that bus trip home, I found his private Facebook.

You can't hide from me, Mister Private Hunk.

And that's when I discovered what I really wanted to know about him. Not the publicity and the famous historic name or where he went to school.

I discovered who Duke Heath-Harding actually was.

The boy was a musician. A saxophonist. He had a selection of cool and arty black-and-white photos of him performing in bars.

So effing cool.

And I could see he could also play other instruments. Piano. Guitar.

He was pretty damn talented, that was for sure. And that probably explained how effortlessly he showed me up with that Didgeridoo.

Oh boy, the man can really work his mouth. And his lips. And his tongue. He must be very… talented in bed…

The bus stopped, and I looked out my window. We were near my flat. The next stop would be mine.

I hovered my finger over his Facebook profile, debating in my head whether to send the man a friend request.

Would that be embarrassing? I guessed I couldn't embarrass myself any more in front of him. Would it seem desperate? I did want to know more about him.

He *was* trying to flirt with me back in the store. Why else would he tenderly hold my chin like that and call me pretty?

I didn't know what to do.

So, I wrote a message to him. Just a draft. Just a way to sort through my thoughts.

Hey! It's me. The embarrassing/pretty girl from the shop with the Didgeridoo that can/cannot work. Wanna be friends?

Yeah, it was pathetic, but I was living my fantasy. A fantasy of marrying a rich handsome Lord with a big country manor and maybe a prize-winning horse or two. Sometimes you gotta let your imagination run wild. Especially after the crazy first day at work I'd had.

I looked up from my seat. I had been so engrossed in my internal argument over whether to send Duke a friend request or not that I hadn't noticed the bus was already at my stop.

And it was about to go.

The engine roared up, and I quickly stood, calling out to the driver.

"Wait, sorry!"

As I reached forward to grab the handrail to balance myself, my finger slipped down my phone. And I did *exactly* what I did not want to do.

I pressed the friend request button.

"Oh God," I exclaimed under my breath.

It was too late to do anything about it now. It had been sent.

And not just the friend request, but the actual freaking message I had deliriously typed out. The stupid little message just meant for me and certainly not for the man I was fantasizing about.

"Oh, God. Grace, you massive twat. Why did you do that for?"

I couldn't delete it. He was going to see it.

It was going to be as embarrassing as my ass in the air, if not even more so.

I held my hand to my head, cringing hard, as I jumped off the bus and headed back home. I berated myself with a whole host of imaginative swear words the entire way down the street to my flat.

I guessed my accidental button press was fate wanting me to do that.

Yeah. Fate. That's how I'll spin it.

"Grace Madden, you are such a loser," I whispered to myself as I pulled out my house key.

Rick - the cockney owner of the fish and chips shop below my flat - gave me an enthusiastic wave through the window as I awkwardly unlocked my front door. I replied with a less-than-enthusiastic wave back.

Duke Heath-Harding was definitely going to read my message, and there was nothing I could do about it.

It was now time to wait for his reply.

5

GRACE

IT HAD BEEN EXACTLY four days, two hours, and fourteen minutes *exactly* since I'd accidentally sent that message to Duke Heath-Harding, and I'd yet to receive a reply.

And it was driving me completely, head-bangingly mad.

Have I completely screwed this up?

At least I had work to go to. Working eased my mind and took it off from thinking about Duke twenty-four hours a day.

Even in my dreams, he was there, somehow even more handsome and gorgeous than in real life. He *dominated* my thoughts. All night, every night, I had dreams about him returning to Small, picking me up from the ground in his rough and strong arms. Kissing me passionately. Taking me into his high-flying billionaire life. I didn't want the money, I just wanted *him*.

Those dreams were longing to escape into reality.

I've really crossed over the edge, haven't I? I've gone full crazy.

On day four of zero contact from Duke, I stood behind the counter at Small and sighed. The man hadn't come back into the store to visit since that day he came in and called me pretty. I knew it was silly, but I did imagine that he might've tried his luck the next day by popping in to say hello, but who was I to think a billionaire bad boy would even spare a moment's thought to that random girl he absentmindedly flirted with in some shop? The memory of me was gone from his mind the moment he stepped out the front door of Small. I was nothing to him.

But I still hung on hope. As I stood behind that counter, I checked my phone again. In case he had messaged me or had even seen my message.

But *no*. Not one word from him.

Getting completely ghosted by Duke was somehow even more embarrassing than my stupid little message.

"If I see that phone in your hands one more time, then I'm throwing it in the bin."

Mabel had dramatically appeared beside me, silent and menacing. Her beady eyes narrowed in anger at the device I was flicking through.

I didn't know why she kept me on at the store if she was so infuriated by me. Maybe it was because I was someone ready to do literally anything she commanded. I needed the job, so I was able to put up with her crap. I was probably the only person in the world who could.

And I also needed to find out if Duke had replied. Mabel had caught me on my phone multiple times that day, checking exactly that, and she was getting rather cross by this point in the evening.

I quickly pocketed the phone and gave her a smile.

"Anything you'll like me to do or help you with, Mabel?"

My boss grumbled something incoherent and strolled back into the office.

Maybe because Duke and I weren't even friends on Facebook that my message just ended up in some online void. Lost. It wasn't like he was ignoring me, surely?

You're deluding yourself, Grace.

I quickly checked the phone one more time. There were no customers in the store and absolutely nothing work-wise for me to do. Mabel was in the back. One fast look wasn't going to hurt, surely?

I dived into Duke's personal profile. My heart beat wildly when I noticed that a new post had popped up on his feed. He was announcing a new performance at some underground jazz bar in Soho.

That very night.

In just a few hours.

If I were to catch him in time, then I would have to leave work very soon. Very, very soon.

Should I go? Should I see him play? I mean, that would be really cool to see even if he has ghosted me.

"Back on your phone again?" Mabel had emerged from her office like a hawk. Her words cut right through the air.

"Is it time to close?" I asked, trying to change the subject before she got even more irate.

"Not just yet," Mabel replied, happy to boast about her plans. "But I am off to an early dinner party right now. I'm looking forward to this one. The Mayor of London shall make an appearance tonight."

"Oh, nice."

"I'm relying on you to lock up again."

She'd told me the day before that I would finish around now. Locking up would take ages. Time I couldn't waste if I wanted the chance to see Duke perform.

This might be my one chance to see him live. The man

rarely did performances. And I couldn't take my mind off him.

I *needed* to see him.

"You did say yesterday that I could finish now," I replied to my boss. "Is that still possible?"

Her lips turned into a sneer. "Well, that's changed. I'm going to this dinner party now, and it's something I can't miss. You're to close up tonight."

"But I do have this thing I was planning to see. Is it possible for me to leave early instead of closing up? I'm happy to stay later any other time this week," I replied, trying to be as sweet and gentle as I could. "I can close every other day, just not tonight."

Mabel stared at me with sheer indignation written on her face.

"Do you want to work here or not, young petulant woman?"

What?

"Are you going to *fire* me if I have to leave now?" I asked. "Are you serious?"

"I am being deadly serious," Mabel replied coldly.

I can't believe what I'm hearing. She's horrible.

"Is that an ultimatum?"

"It's your choice," Mabel replied with a smirk. "Leave now and never come back. Or follow my order and stay."

She then aggressively threw the keys towards me like she'd done the other day, thinking I would just blindly follow her commands.

But I was tired of being treated like trash.

I had put up with Mabel's shit for nearly a week. I needed a job, but I wasn't this desperate.

And I really wanted to see Duke.

I caught the keys and immediately threw them back at her. She fumbled to catch them.

"I guess I'm leaving, then," I replied sternly. "See you, Mabel. Well, I guess I won't see you ever again now, won't I?"

Oh boy, you should've seen the look on her face.

Priceless.

But I couldn't savor it for long. I had a handsome musician to see.

6

GRACE

I WAS ELATED.

The bright lights of the nightclubs and small bars of London's Soho sparkled like stars in the puddles on the cobblestone streets. I carefully avoided the growing pools of water as I skipped through the pouring rain across the narrow streets towards the underground jazz club where Duke was due to perform that night. I held my umbrella close to my head.

Don't get wet. Don't get wet.

People out for a good drunken night passed me as I made my way around the puddles. Soho was busy, the night attracting those wanting to lose themselves in booze, music, and dancing.

I was one of those people, nerves titillating me as I reached the door leading down into the basement of the jazz club. The thought that very soon I'd be seeing Duke Heath-Harding perform sent my body on edge. In a good, exciting way.

"You alright?" the bouncer on the front doors asked me as I approached.

I gave him a nod and showed him my ID. He let me through.

I was greeted by a small room surrounded by bookcases. It appeared I had reached a dead-end, but I knew what to do.

The only way to get downstairs was to push against one of the bookcases. A pulley system worked, and the bookcase swung open into a hidden staircase.

"Cool," I whispered.

This place was properly secretive, and that thrilled me.

The jazz club was located right in the heart of Soho. I loved the hustle and bustle of the West End. This was my part of town.

I tied up my dripping umbrella and headed down the stairs, balancing myself on the handrail as I descended underground.

The club itself was *tiny*. In the best kind of fashion. The bar ran into the audience space. Chairs were all within an arm's reach of each other. It invoked fantasies of a thirties New York speakeasy. The room would've been in complete darkness if it weren't for dim red and blue lights illuminating the walls and stage, giving the place an undercover feel.

Mirrors hung on every wall. I caught a glimpse of myself.

When I left Small - for possibly the last ever time - I made a beeline straight for home, where I got quickly changed. I found a dark blue dress I hadn't worn for years but which perfectly fitted my eyes. For the main event, I went into the bathroom and generously applied a bright red shade of lipstick. I would never have usually had the confidence to use such a striking color, but that night I was feeling adventurous. I wanted to stand out.

If I was going to see Duke's performance, then I wanted him to notice me.

Oh, he definitely will with this kind of lipstick on.

In the jazz club, I ordered a drink at the bar. A glass of white wine. And then I took a seat by the side of the stage.

This is so exciting.

The place was so cramped that, when I sat in the chair, my knees were practically on the small stage. No one was up there yet, just a piano and drum kit sitting empty.

I wonder how long it would be before Duke's in front of me.

My legs quivered with excitement at what was to come. Would he really notice me? Would he spot me in the crowd?

Does he even want to see me again?

I felt so exposed coming there on my own. Like applying that bright red lipstick, I would never have done something so bold as to go alone to a jazz club. But I really was feeling a strong *fuck it* attitude that night. I'd embarrassed myself already in front of Duke, so doing it again didn't mean a thing.

Sometimes in life, you gotta live out your fantasies. You gotta let yourself bathe in a dream. Indulge yourself. And that was exactly what I was doing that night.

I was all alone, so I pulled out the novel I was currently reading. Just to appear like I was calm and confident, which I most certainly wasn't on the inside.

My throat was dry, and I couldn't sit still.

I was reading Wuthering Heights. An old favorite of my mother's. She used to read it to me as a bedtime story when I was a kid, and I loved it. I definitely got my crazy side from her.

If only she could see me now. She'd love what I'm doing tonight.

It was not long after I had opened up the tattered paperback when the bar went quiet. The scattered audience took their seats.

And then the show began.

A man I did not recognize appeared on stage first, and then another. They picked up instruments. One went on the piano. One pulled up a trumpet. Another man sat behind the drum kit.

And then Duke strolled on stage with all the casual swagger he'd entered into the shop the other day.

And my heart stopped.

It seemed to not start beating again until after his smooth voice spoke into the microphone, introducing the other men on stage, and then he picked up a saxophone.

I had to remind myself to breathe as I watched him. Duke was dressed in a sharp black suit. The man was so effortlessly stylized. He could wear anything and look just damn effing *cool*.

He brought the saxophone to his lips and began to play.

Here we bloody go.

The next half hour was a glorious display of jazz. I had never been into that genre of music, nor had spent much time listening to it, but I could spend all night listening to Duke perform. The music rocked my body. My focus did not fall from the musicians on stage. The untouched wine in my glass went warm in my hands as I sat, captivated.

The sexy man was so close to me that I could reach out with no effort at all and touch him if I had only dared to.

Surely he can recognize me? Recognize my face sitting so close in the audience?

His eyes never found me, and that tore my insides to pieces. I was so nervous about him spotting me and yet I did not want to leave without him acknowledging me. It was like I was there searching for an answer. I wanted him to want me.

Does that sound crazy?

It probably does, but I probably am crazy.

Then the music was over - seemingly as quickly as it had begun - and the musicians stepped off the stage to disappear behind a dark curtain.

Duke was gone.

He hadn't even looked at me once during the whole show, and now I was left sitting in my seat cupping a warm glass of wine.

Maybe he hadn't noticed me. Maybe he'd forgotten my face as soon as he'd left Small.

Maybe I was just being a silly little heart-stricken girl to go to that jazz club that night.

Maybe I should just go home.

But then someone was behind me, leaning over my shoulder. I smelled the familiar mixture of amber and citrus before I saw him.

Duke...

As I turned in my chair to face him, he was already saying my name in that deep, sexy voice of his.

"Hello, Grace."

7

GRACE

"Can I sit down?"

Duke stood so close to me and all I could think about were his soft lips forming those words. The whole world faded from view and all that was left was the tall handsome man in the tight, expensive suit and that dark curly hair of his that hung so deliciously down over his brow.

I nodded in response, unable to speak.

I was frozen in place. At least I was sitting down and holding onto my wine glass for dear life. He couldn't see how much I really wanted to quiver in nervousness.

As he sat down next to me - our knees gently brushing - my head repeated one sentence over and over.

He has noticed me.

"You remember me?" Duke asked softly. The rest of the bar was loud with post-show audience conversations but, with his voice directed at me in that quiet, intense way, it felt like the only people existing in this place were him and me and no one else.

I bit my lower lip and squinted, pretending to think for a moment. Pretending to not recognize that beautiful face so close to mine.

"Oh. Right. It's *you* from the shop the other day."

He smiled coyly. I didn't know whether he was laughing at me for my bad performance at not remembering him or that he genuinely thought I had somehow forgotten who he was. "Duke. Duke Heath-Harding."

Fuck me. The way he says his name is like pouring heat into my pussy.

"Yes, that's your name. I'm Grace."

"I remember," he replied. "The girl with the ass in the air."

"Ugh, let's never talk about that."

"Sure. What are you doing here, Grace?"

I nonchalantly waved my hand around the bar. "I just thought of seeing some jazz."

Duke's eyebrow raised. "You decided to watch some jazz *alone*?"

"Yep."

"On a Friday night?"

"Yeah."

He shook his head and remained silent for a moment, thinking. I could see the cogs turning behind his bright blue eyes. "Right."

"So, you recognized me?" I asked, my voice barely registering higher than a whisper.

"Of course I recognized you."

"Really?"

"Well, apart from your lipstick. It's very red. Very... *striking*."

"It is."

He moved in closer, then. Our mouths were mere inches away.

"I like it, though," he said. He gestured towards the stage. "Did you like the show?"

"It was alright."

He raised an eyebrow. "Just alright?"

"The saxophonist was a bit off, I thought."

Duke leaned even closer.

"One thing you should know about me, Grace, is that I don't take kindly to criticism. Even if it's in jest."

"Why would you think I'm joking? I'm giving my honest opinion."

He snarled at me. A wild look flashed in his eyes.

I've stirred the beast within.

"You're a tough woman to please, aren't you?"

"I've heard that before."

Duke's eyes flickered down to my bag.

"Wuthering Heights?" he asked, curious.

My book was partially pulled out of my bag. When his band had started, I didn't get enough time to put it in properly.

And now Duke had seen it.

"Yeah. I'm reading it."

"Interesting. You like it?"

"This is not my first time reading it."

"You didn't answer my question, Grace. I asked if you like it."

"If I didn't, then why would I be reading it again?"

"Touché. So, you like your dark heroes, then?" Duke asked, hushed. Like our conversation was a secret that no one else should hear. "Do you, Grace? You like your bad boys with an ice-cold heart? Upon the windy moors with no one else around to tell you to stop as you fall in love?"

A chill went up my whole body as he spoke.

I shrugged, though. Holding back all that raging desire within me to just reach out and kiss this dark man. I knew the way he was speaking to me was not new to him. I bet he did this with all the girls, but it still sent a rush through me that was simply irresistible to not bask in.

This was a man who knew how to handle himself. A man just like Heathcliff. A man who didn't take no for an answer and pursued his love, even if it took him across the world to get her.

Duke was a man ripped from the pages of a windswept Gothic novel.

And that turned me on as no man had done before.

"It's pretty good, I guess."

That was my reply. It was the understatement of the century, but I didn't want Duke to think that all he had to say were some dark words and I'd fall irrevocably into his lap.

"Oh, I didn't know I was dealing with a real literary critic here," he said.

"You're dealing with a lot more than that," I replied, before standing up and taking a step back from him. "Excuse me, I'm going to the bathroom."

"You're excused."

Duke smiled as I slowly turned and headed towards the ladies. I sensed his eyes drift down to my lower back as I strolled away. Without a doubt, he was taking in my ass.

It was exactly right where I wanted him.

I left him to sit there next to the stage and think about me. Only me. I wanted him to want *more* of me. To be begging for more.

In the bathroom, I washed my hands. They were shaking, but I knew I'd done a good performance out there. A better performance than Duke had done on his shiny saxophone.

There was no one else in there with me. Just me and my thoughts.

You've got him curled around your finger, Grace. You've tamed a wild animal there.

I glanced up into the mirror to check my red lipstick.

And in the reflection, I saw Duke standing behind me. He took a step into the bathroom and shut the door behind him. We were alone.

8

GRACE

I DIDN'T TURN around to face Duke. Instead, I glared at his reflection behind me in the mirror.

"You can't be in here," I said, my voice firm. "This is the ladies' loo."

Duke scowled and took three slow steps towards me so that his broad chest was practically rubbing right up against the back of my neck.

Oh, he does not give a fuck.

My skin shivered at his proximity. My body flipped to high alert.

There was no one else in there, no one in the bathroom to witness Duke lean down to my ear so that his soft lips brushed lightly against my neck. I still refused to turn around and face him, preferring to put up my defenses and glare back at him through the mirror.

But his tender touch was tearing through my coldness like a hot knife cutting butter.

"I can do whatever the fuck I want," he whispered into

my ear, his searing breath pouring into me like liquid. "Do you not know? I am Duke Heath-Harding."

I crumbled under his voice.

And then I felt his hands grip my waist. I let go of any resistance and allowed the muscular man to spin me around to face him. His lips were right in my eyeline. Thick and full.

Jesus.

I let out a soft moan, and he dragged me in close. He was so strong. Muscular. Overpowering.

His consuming, manly scent enveloped me, and I was like putty in his hands.

And then he claimed my lips with a kiss.

Despite the boundless strength in his arms holding me tight, his kiss was gentle. Seductive. He was pulling me in with his hungry touch, and I couldn't do a thing to stop him. I didn't *want* to stop him.

"Oh, I really like those lips of yours," Duke said as he drew back from me, staring at my face with those piercing blue eyes. "That color is *everything*."

"Thank you," I managed to reply. I felt that, even if I collapsed under the weight of his intense stare, he'd manage to catch me. He wouldn't let me fall. I was completely surrounded by Duke. His thick arms wrapped around my waist.

But I still didn't want to give in to him completely. Sure, I was *kissing* him in the ladies' bathroom with the door shut, but I didn't want to be just some girl fawning over the rich playboy. I wanted him to *work* to get me.

"I might head home," I said, maintaining my eye contact. "It's been a long night."

Duke took my chin between his fingers just as he had done the other day at Small and kissed me again.

Damn, this boy is smooth.

"I really gotta go," I said as our lips parted.

Duke merely slightly smiled.

"Sure."

He released me from his grip, and I headed out of the bathroom and back up the stairs. I didn't dare glance behind.

If he desired me, then he would have to find me.

I had left enough clues to find out who I was. This time it was up to him to play detective.

But I didn't have to wait for long for Duke to chase me. He was already beside me on the pavement outside the jazz club before I could walk around the corner.

"Where are you going?" he asked me. He must've bounded up those stairs to reach me so quickly.

The rain was lighter now. The streets were busy, but now everyone was staggering around, drunk.

"I'm walking home," I replied, continuing to walk away from the club down Soho's streets illuminated by LED shop lights. Duke stayed beside me at my pace. "I might get the Tube. We'll see."

"I'm not letting you walk home at this time of night," he replied. "Not through Soho. Not in the dark."

Before I could reply and tell him that I could handle myself perfectly well, *thank you very much*, he had already raised his hand in the air and whistled a black cab down. The car stopped alongside us.

"Get in."

He was so firm, so fucking insistent with his eyes that I could not turn him down.

"Fine," I replied. "If you're paying."

Duke smiled. "You've got a fire in you, don't you?"

"You haven't seen the least of it yet," I replied before sliding into the backseat of the taxi. I told the driver my flat's address as Duke sat down right next to me.

The feel of his body against mine sent me into overdrive.

And then the taxi started, and we headed down London's night-time streets with only the music of the radio playing.

What is even happening to me?

My fantasies were coming true.

In the darkness of the cab, Duke's hand found mine, and he gripped it tight.

"You're not coming to mine, are you?" I asked the man.

"No."

"Good, because there wasn't an invite."

"I'm a gentleman, Grace. I don't invite myself over on the first date. I'm just making sure you get home okay."

"So, this is a date?"

Duke's blue eyes found mine in the darkness of the cab.

"What do you think this is, Grace?" he asked me.

Was this a date? Because it was not like any other date I had ever been on. There was a spark. A delicious tension between us.

I would never do anything like this, but I was a little tipsy, and he was so *freaking* gorgeous.

And my body was in heat.

I needed this.

"This was just meant to be me enjoying a little bit of jazz," I said. "It certainly *wasn't* a date."

"Enjoying a bit of jazz on your own?"

"Yep."

"On a Friday night?"

"Yep."

"In the same small bar in Soho where I perform?"

"Yep. What a coincidence."

"It really is," Duke replied. "Grace, you really are an enigma, aren't you?"

I looked at him.

"I am."

He smiled. "And I like that."

"Do you usually go into strange little shops in Notting Hill?" I asked him.

"I don't make a habit of it," he replied. "Only when there are pretty assistants working there."

There was that word again. *Pretty.* I couldn't help but feel a flutter of warmth flood through me as the word left his gorgeous lips.

We fell into a silence. I looked out the window at the city passing by, trying hard not to continue lustfully staring at Duke.

This night can't be real.

"You don't mind if I check my emails?" the man asked me.

"Go ahead."

Beside me, Duke pulled out his phone. I saw him open his social media apps.

Facebook. Not his email.

And then he was into his messages.

Mine was on top.

He clicked on it.

Read it without a word.

Turned to me.

Oh, God.

"Now I'm truly embarrassed," I said, my cheeks blushing a deeper red than my lipstick. What a *perfect* moment for him to read my silly message for the first time.

If Duke was weirded out by the whole thing, then he didn't show it. He remained perfectly calm. His face unrevealing.

He took his time to slowly lean over my shoulder,

heading straight for my ear, just like he did back in the jazz club's bathroom. A shiver passed through me as I remembered how he had taken my lips.

I thought he was going to kiss me again, but he didn't.

I certainly wasn't ready for what he asked me next, which he delivered in his ice-cold, smooth voice.

"I think you lied to me, Grace. You didn't just turn up to the jazz club on a whim, didn't you?"

9

GRACE

DUKE MADE me squirm in my seat. His hand gripped mine even tighter.

"I did not lie to you *exactly*," I answered back.

"What? So, you wanted to see some jazz and just happened to stumble across me four days after you sent that message?"

Damn. I had to admit that Duke had me there.

There was no point in hiding from him anymore. He knew exactly what I was after when I came dressed like that with *that* lipstick all the way across town to the jazz club.

Him.

He'd found me out.

And now I was stuck in the backseat of a cab with him.

I wasn't complaining.

Duke leaned in closer.

"You know what I do with liars?" he asked me quietly. Menacingly.

"No," I gasped back. I really wanted to hear what this man would do with me.

I didn't have to wait long.

"I punish them."

Holy shit.

He let go of my hand.

My body shuddered as his fingers made their way up the inside of my thigh. Up my dress.

I kept my face forward as to not reveal how much just the tip of his hand was making me feel. I didn't want the taxi driver to suspect a thing.

But my body was on fire. A line of juice ran down from my pussy, coating Duke's fingers. He grinned at me as he felt my wetness, enjoying how dangerous this secretive act was in the back of this taxi.

But Duke Heath-Harding didn't care how bad he was being.

His hand crawled up under my dress even further.

He *was* right. He was punishing me.

I wanted to scream in pleasure, but all I allowed myself to let out was a tiny sigh of delight. That caused Duke's hand to work even closer to my wet pussy. He didn't touch me where I desired to be touched just yet. No, he was not going to give in that easily. He knew exactly how much he was teasing me; it was clear in the gleam of his blue eyes in the dark. He was hauling me to the point of climax.

Oh, God...

And then his hand retreated back from between my legs. He yanked it out from under my dress.

I uttered an involuntary groan as the growing pleasure he was building up inside me was left uncompleted. I *burned* for him.

"Change of address," he said, turning to the driver. "We're going back to mine."

I didn't have the energy anymore to protest.

I didn't even want to.

Duke had brought me to the point of climax, it was only fair that he finished the job he started.

This man knows exactly what he is doing.

* * *

THE NEXT FEW minutes flew by in a blur. I don't even remember the taxi arriving at Duke's building, only that I definitely made my way inside some plush reception place, and then into some lift up to a top penthouse. And then his front door.

And then his lips.

I was consumed by the man. Drawn to him like a moth to a flame. My entire body lusted for him with every fiber of my being.

"You can't tease me like that and not fuck me," I whispered to him in the dark of his apartment.

"I told you that you deserve to be punished," he retorted darkly.

"You've punished me enough. Why else do you think I've come back here? Now you have to finish the job."

That was his turn to moan. Oh, I loved how he was being turned on by my demand.

My surroundings didn't matter, only Duke did. Only his impossibly chiseled face dominated my sight.

"Oh, you want me to fuck you?" Duke asked, his voice barely above a whisper. "You naughty little shop assistant."

I nodded. Once. Twice.

I really want to be fucked.

And then he was undressing me. His hands removed the straps of my bra, and they found my nipples, already erect by how turned on I was by the way he was posses-sively looking at me.

I didn't let his hands get any further.

"Let me see you," I whisper as my fingers clawed at his shirt's buttons, ripping them off one by one. "I want to see what you look like under your suit."

My god, his chest did *not* disappoint.

"You're feisty, aren't you?" Duke asked, and I bit my lip. He took that as permission to push me down on his massive bed. "Give me your hands."

I raised my wrists to him as Duke reached under his bed. He was getting something from down there. I realized what it was when I felt rope around my hands.

He was tying me up.

And it was so goddamn sexy.

Oh.

I squealed and Duke's thumb quickly found my open mouth, immediately silencing me.

"Be quiet," he commanded me in his deep, sensual voice. "You need to be punished, bad girl."

I nodded eagerly, my eyes wide. I was loving this. I was loving being treated like a naughty little girl.

Duke was firm as he tied me up, but also gentle. He knew exactly what strength to apply as he dominated my body.

His finger traced around the edge of my soaking wet pussy again, and I found myself whining against his thumb in my mouth.

It's not fair how much he can tease me like this.

My legs shuddered and my hands struggled in vain against their restraints. I looked up to see Duke grinning in triumph over my naked and tied-up body.

Oh, that goddamn smile.

That sent me over the edge. I cried out in pure ecstasy

as my pussy surged in an orgasm that filled me up with pleasure.

"Are you sufficiently punished?" Duke asked me as I squirmed in delight against the rope. "Are you a good girl yet? Have you learned your lesson that you shouldn't follow me, you naughty little stalker?"

He removed his thumb from my mouth so that I could speak.

"Nope."

That was my reply, and Duke seemed to really enjoy it.

He ripped down his suit pants so that his cock sprung out. It was so goddamn massive. I gasped at the sight of it.

"I guess I've got to really drill it into you, then," Duke snarled before he climbed on top of me and thrust his immense member inside of my wet pussy.

I gulped as he filled me with his cock.

Somehow, this was even more thrilling than how he used his fingers moments before. He was so deep inside my willing pussy. So hard and strong. My hands were so restrained that they couldn't even push him off me if I tried.

And I certainly didn't want him to get off me.

Waves of pleasure swelled through me again as I experienced another climax.

Wow.

Duke continued to plow into me. I felt my body gearing up to ride another crest of bliss. He wasn't going to rest until he had wrung every bit of pleasure from me. He wanted to see me beg for him to stop. For it to get too much for me to bear.

And that's when I knew then that this night was going to last for a very long time.

And I wasn't complaining. Not at all.

10

GRACE

I woke up in Duke's bed next to the sleeping body of the man feeling absolutely on top of the bloody world.

I glanced around the room. I hadn't had much time to check out the man's apartment properly last night. My attention was, shall we say... *elsewhere*.

But now, in the light of a sunny London morning, I could really inspect the place.

Duke lived in a fancy penthouse, that was for sure. I didn't expect anywhere else for such a wealthy aristocrat. The decor screamed a man with expensive taste. The walls were adorned with cool, minimalistic artwork. Paintings with just a simple brush of color. I bet he paid a lot for those things. Floor-to-ceiling glass windows looking out over London surrounded me.

With a gulp, I realized his bedroom must've been nearly the same size as my entire flat.

This can't be possible. No one's this rich.

I'd never seen my home city from this angle before.

His bedsheets were smooth and silky. I loved falling asleep wrapped in them.

It was even better to fall asleep next to Duke himself with his arms cuddling me in close.

I turned to the still-sleeping man and poked him awake. I certainly wasn't going to lie there all morning waiting for him to wake up like a little obedient wife.

He slowly blinked open his blue eyes, focusing his attention on me. Just the way I liked.

"Morning," he croaked in a deep, just-awake, sexy voice.

"Morning you," I replied. My heart pounded in my chest.

"Last night was fun."

I nodded and shifted in close to him. His massive bicep curled around my neck, drawing me in even closer. His body was so warm.

Duke's hand drifted down to cup my bare ass. I bit my lower lip as my pussy began to wake up to his touch.

"Yeah, it was fun."

"I liked how you came to visit me," he whispered. "You're the sexiest stalker I've ever had."

"I told you I just wanted to watch some jazz. The last thing I wanted to do was to end up here."

Duke smiled sleepily, not believing my flimsy story.

"Sure, sure," he replied. "But you must admit that running into me was the best part of your night."

"Maybe."

"Oh, you tease."

"You know me," I replied.

"I actually don't know you," he said quietly. There was a brief pause before he uttered his next line. "It would be good to get to know you, though."

Good to get to know me?

"Is that what you say to all the girls?"

He smirked. "Maybe."

"I bet you do this all the time."

"You can read my mind now, Grace?"

He was being playful with me, and I was enjoying it, but I was still nervous about what he was saying. Maybe it was true. Maybe he did do this with a lot of girls. I wouldn't be surprised. A rich gorgeous bachelor living in the middle of a world-class city. Of course, there would be girls lining up around the block with their panties down for him.

"How about you treat me to breakfast first?" I suggested. "Then you can get to know me more."

"Sounds perfect," Duke replied as he leaned forward to kiss me delicately on the lips. "I need to have a shower first."

"But I'm hungry."

He winked at me before throwing off the bedsheets and leaping out of bed. "Shower first and then breakfast."

Warmth flooded my pussy as I greedily surveyed his muscular and *very naked* frame as he headed to his bathroom.

The man was too good to be real.

Had I dreamed last night? It certainly felt like a fantasy I might've come up with as I played with my clit in bed.

No. Last night was very real, Grace. Your pussy wouldn't still be quivering with delight the next morning if that didn't happen.

The shower began in the next room, and I decided it was my time to go snooping around.

I wasn't being *too* bad. Okay, maybe just a tiny bit. A naughty girl. Maybe I deserved to be punished again? I would very much like that.

The way he tied me up...

I just wished to understand this man I'd slept with a little bit more. Was that so harsh?

My sexiest stalker.

That's what he'd said. Well, now it was time to live up to that mantel.

Wearing one of Duke's shirts, which was about forty sizes too big for me and stretched down to my knees - *the man was so incredibly broad-shouldered* - I tiptoed out of the bedroom into the living room of the penthouse. The apartment was so goddamn nice. It was like one of those places you see online that's a celebrity's house on sale, and you just salivate thinking about living there whilst knowing you never could.

I felt like I shouldn't even belong there, that I'd been dropped into some show home and some person with a clipboard might appear at any moment to usher me out.

There was more fancy modern art on the perfectly white walls in the living room. The sofas were of an amazing make. The kitchen was sparse, with only the best utensils hanging.

"Wow," I whispered in awe.

I spotted some photo frames sitting on top of a shelf. I immediately checked them out. I would've very much liked to have seen some photos of Duke's family, and here was my chance. Of course, I wouldn't stop snooping now.

All the images were of Duke. In one, he was standing next to two young children. A boy and a girl. In another, he was playing in a park with them and a woman around our age smiling on.

And another photo was of him with the same woman. Except this one didn't have kids in it. This one was of the woman wearing a wedding dress and Duke was wearing a suit.

And they were holding each other lovingly. Smiling into the camera. A perfect image of a happy couple in love.

I gasped.

Something heavy formed in the pit of my stomach. Dread.

I have slept with a married man.

These were photos he'd kept away from social media. Trust me, I would never have slept with Duke if I'd known he was married, and I certainly wouldn't have even dared go to the jazz club if I'd known he had a family.

It all made sense. He *was* too good to be real. There was always going to be a catch.

What have I done?

I spun around to the bedroom. The shower was still running. Duke was still in the bathroom with no clue as to what I've just seen.

This was my chance to go. I was not going to wait around in this apartment anymore. I didn't want to hear his pathetic reasoning behind last night. I was sure the man was full of excuses.

Liar.

Was this penthouse a place he kept secret from his family? Was this a place the married man brought home girls he picked up?

How could I have been so stupid?

I should've checked he wasn't married. I was so focused on snaring this handsome man that I didn't even think to find out more about him.

And now I had potentially ruined another woman's life.

That was it. I had enough. I walked straight out the front door of Duke's penthouse looking - *and definitely feeling* - dirty and messy.

A girl used.

I was upset. I was angry. No, I was fucking *pissed*.

The very first thing I did when I walked out of his apartment building was to block Duke on everything. Social media. His number.

Everything.

Cheating bastard. I should never have fallen for him. I should've been more bloody wary.

I promised myself right then and there that I would never see that man again.

11

PRESENT DAY

GRACE

I HAD TOLD myself I wouldn't see Duke Heath-Harding ever again, but that silly little promise only lasted four years.

But four years later and I'm a different woman. I've grown up since I was a naïve little eighteen-year-old, falling immediately head-over-heels with a rich playboy who'd once flirted with me for ten minutes in a shop. Now I am more experienced. I know myself. I have boundaries.

I don't put up with anyone's bullshit. Especially a man's.

That experience with Duke taught me a valuable lesson. I would not be played with like that again. I've promised myself that no man will ever take me for a ride like Duke had done.

Four years later is when I decide - rather bravely and perhaps a little stupidly - to break into the theater Scarlett works at. I'm only there to investigate the murder of Kingsley's publicist that happened on the stage only a few weeks ago. The theater hasn't been opened since, and the police have barred it up. It's a dark and scary place now that no one's inside.

I come to give the place a look around, and that's when I give both Scarlett and me the fright of our lives.

I'm a big true crime nut. Like a freaking *massive* one. I watch everything to do with real murders and serial killers and crimes. I'm crazy about it.

And, hey, it's not like I'm in love with any murderers. I'm not like one of those women who camped outside Ted Bundy's prison and wrote long letters to him. I'm just super fascinated by human nature, that's all. I want to know why these men would go and kill another human being in cold blood. What drove them to do that? What did they hope to gain?

Someone had murdered King's publicist in the same way a serial killer might've done, and that sent my senses into alarm. I've done enough research to spot a serial killer a mile away, and I knew this man would strike again.

And it could be someone I know.

Especially after he'd threatened King.

This murderer was going after people I care about. I might as well put years of obsessively watching endless crime documentaries to good use.

And that's why I've broken into the Prestige Theater, to investigate what happened so that maybe we could get the upper hand on this asshole. It might sound optimistically misplaced and arrogant, but maybe I can find something the police haven't found.

I've practically got the training after all those hours in front of the TV.

And that's when I surprise Scarlett. And she surprised me.

She lets out a scream - standing in the middle of the stage - when she sees me emerge from the darkness of backstage.

And her scream causes me to scream.

So we both stand there, screaming at each other.

Bloody hell.

"Scarlett?"

"Grace?"

"What the hell are you doing here?"

"I could ask you the exact same thing."

"I'm investigating," Scarlett says.

"So am I," I reply.

"We're such doofuses," Scarlett snorts, and I laugh.

"Total idiots."

We run to hug each other, laughing our heads off. I guess I can say we're both pretty happy that the other isn't a murderer in the dark.

"What are we even doing here?" Scarlett asks me, shaking her head.

"I'm just trying to help the investigation," I reply. "But now I feel completely stupid. And useless."

"So do I," Scarlett agrees. "I don't know why I thought I could do a better job than a professional police detective."

"Me too. I just thought that with all the crap I watch on TV that I might have some skills, but apparently, all I'm good at is for scaring you."

"I do love how we both thought of doing the same thing," she says.

"*Twinsies*," I joke.

Scarlett playfully slaps me on the arm and shoots me a disapproving frown at the word.

Right, to be fair, I might be here because of the murder. But I might also be here because I kinda want to run into Duke again. When I found out he is King's brother the other morning, I experienced every emotion one could possibly experience when they see a ghost from the past. Anger. Betrayal. Fear.

And a little bit of excitement.

The man used me, but he was so goddamn gorgeous. He might've been married when we slept together and I might hate his guts for lying to me about that, but that night has remained imprinted in my mind like nothing else since. No other man has ever compared to how Duke had pleasured me that time four years ago. I've not thought of any man more than I thought of Duke.

So. Yeah. I don't ever want to see that man again.

But. Also. I kinda *do*.

I must be crazy.

I don't know what I want. I guess that's my problem. I guess that's why every relationship I've had with a man seems to fuck up.

I've been searching for another Duke Heath-Harding for four years - without the whole *having an affair* thing - but nothing compares to the original.

"Let's get out of this dark, scary theater," Scarlett suggests. "I don't want to get startled again."

I nod. "Absolutely."

"Let's go to King's. We'll tell him about this."

Of course Scarlett wants us to go to her boyfriend's place.

All I'm thinking of is one thing. There's a very high chance that *he* will be there.

My fucked-up wish might actually be coming true. I might break that promise I made to myself four years ago.

I'm going to see Duke again.

12

DUKE

"So, what really is happening with the police? Have they said anything to you about this prick who sent them that letter?"

My brother doesn't react straight away. He takes a long time to answer, gripping the back of the chair and sighing.

"No. They've been pretty useless, if I may say so. They haven't told me what to do."

He clenches his jaw and avoids eye contact with me. I know my brother well enough to tell that he's extremely uncomfortable with this conversation. I know he feels like he doesn't need me to go over this with him, but I truly must.

His life is at stake here.

"They haven't offered protection?" My voice begins to rise, and it rarely does that. I am usually a very calm man, but right now I am angry. How dare the police act like this is all nothing.

A man has made a threat against King's life, and the police are not doing a damn thing.

But my brother doesn't seem as affected by it as I am. It's like he's got the same attitude as the police. Business as normal. He sighs and then shrugs. Like he's shrugging off the threat as if it's bloody nothing and not the most serious thing he's ever faced.

"I'll have to do everything myself, but it's no matter."

"No matter? This is fucking important, King. You have to take this seriously." I make my way towards King's alcohol cabinet and pull out a rare unopened bottle of Scotch. This one is worth a few thousand pounds. Pocket money for King and me.

I only ever drink the best.

"We will sort this out," my brother replies, watching me pour us both a glass of the Scotch. "We always face any challenge and win. We're Heath-Harding boys."

I hand him a glass. "That we are, King. I worry about you, brother. Even at school, I looked out for you. Anyone who tried to challenge you would have to fight their way for me, and it's just the same now. We're blood, and I'm not willing to let this prick come between us. I'm prepared to shed his own blood to protect my younger brother."

"Cheers to that," King says and chinks my glass with his own.

We drink.

The liquid is strong and tough, just like us. We've been through a lot, King and me. We're stronger than any asshole murderer.

I turn to look out the view from King's penthouse. His place is right above Tower Bridge. London's skyline twinkles in the setting sun. The lights on all the buildings slowly come alive, giving the city an otherworldly feel.

"What are you going to do?" I ask my brother, taking another sip of the razor-sharp liquor.

"I'm going to nail the bastard."

"Good."

"The last thing I'm going to let happen is to allow this guy to harm Scarlett."

I raise an eyebrow.

"Your new fling?"

"She's way more than just a fling," King replies sternly. "She's the best thing that's ever happened to me. She is my world. I love that girl more than anyone else on this godforsaken planet."

I smile. "Even me?"

King chuckles and turns away. He's pretty used to my brotherly banter by now. We might fight and mock each other, but we have the other's back. We'll lay down our lives for the other without a moment's hesitation. Our whole lives we've come to rely on only each other, so this Scarlett girl must really mean a hell of a lot to King. He would never joke around about how much he loves someone unless things were mighty serious.

I can see by his face that things are *definitely* serious.

Scarlett is one hell of a lucky woman.

I know, without a doubt, King would do anything for her. Lay down his life for her, just as he would for me.

That makes only two people in the whole world that he would do that for.

I've never had someone like that. I thought I did, though. Once. A long time ago.

But that never worked out.

King will never know how deeply jealous I am of him. Ever since he met Scarlett, he has completely changed. It's like she's lit a spark in him that burns brighter every day. She compliments him like rain comes with thunder.

God, I need a girl like that.

I nearly finish the glass of Scotch. It's good to talk to King about this threat. I know he needs me here, with him. Even if it's just to talk nonsense and drink.

As he said, we'll nail the bastard. Together.

We just have to work as one unit and keep his woman safe in the process. No one will be a match for our combined brainpower and material resources.

"If this asshole even lays one finger on my girl," King mutters. "Then I am coming after him with everything I've got. I won't rest until his head is on a spike on Tower Bridge."

"That's very medieval of you, King."

"By the time I'm done with him, he'll be wishing he was living in the dark ages."

There's suddenly a knock on the door.

I immediately clench my fists, ready. There's no way a murderer could get up here to King's penthouse through security and then just *knock*, but you never know.

We're both on high alert until King looks through the door's peephole.

"It's Scarlett," he says to me, and my body relaxes.

It's good to know she's still safe.

King opens the door for his girlfriend. She storms in, red hair like a blaze behind her. I can see why my brother likes her. She's feisty and pretty. A good combination to nail down a Heath-Harding boy.

"Hi Duke," she says, nodding at me.

"Hello, Scarlett."

We met for the first time the other day.

"You alright?" King asks her.

"You wouldn't have guessed where I've just been." Her voice is crackling with excitement.

"Where?"

"The Prestige Theater."

King's face immediately drops. "What the fuck were you doing there?"

"Investigating."

"No. Scarlett, that isn't safe..."

She cuts him off.

"I can handle myself pretty well, thank you very much."

"But still. Scarlett. I need you here safe with me."

She ignores his protests.

"And then I bumped into my flatmate."

"Grace?" King asks.

"Yeah, she's here too. She came with me."

Scarlett gestures at the open doorway. In steps a girl.

The first thing I notice is how pretty she is.

The next thing I notice is that I've met her before.

Oh, I've *definitely* met her before.

Grace?

The Grace?

I nearly drop my glass of Scotch.

13

DUKE

What is she doing here?

The first thing I notice about Grace Madden is that she looks slightly older, but I guess that's what happens after four years apart.

The next thing I notice is how fucking insanely beautiful she is. Not that I need reminding. I was utterly spellbound by her the first time we met. If only she knew back then how she'd caught me by complete surprise in that Notting Hill shop. How tongue-tied I really was when she spoke to me as I entered the store. I do think I hid it well. It certainly helped that she was more embarrassed by her pretty little ass in the air than to spot how smitten I was for her at first sight.

And now she's somehow even more beautiful.

Jesus Christ.

Those steely little light blue eyes under that raven black wavy hair of hers. That pale smooth skin. That proud way she holds her mouth like she's always ready to fight.

I could take her in my hands and kiss her right now.

She's the girl I remember. Just a lot tougher now. And more experienced. And just as jaw-droppingly gorgeous as the day I first lay my eyes on her.

No wonder I nearly drop my Scotch glass at the sight of her.

"Oh, you two don't know each other," King says, turning his head between Grace and me. He clearly doesn't suspect what's already gone on between us. I bet he would be laughing for days if he did. "Grace, this is my brother, Duke. This is Scarlett's flatmate, Grace."

Wait, did I hear that right? Scarlett's flatmate?

That's who she is?

That explains a lot. That explains why she's in this penthouse. Why Scarlett brought her along.

As my brother introduces us, Grace stares back at me with a stony expression. I can't read her face at all. I wonder if she's as shocked at seeing me as I am of her. I'm impressed at how calm she's taking this all in.

Like she did nothing wrong.

Like she didn't disappear four years ago.

I raise my hand to King to silence him, but I don't take my eyes off the girl standing just a few feet away.

"We already know each other," I reply coolly to my brother.

King frowns. "You two? How?"

Scarlett doesn't say a word. Neither does Grace.

Something is wrong here.

They both know about me. They both knew that I'd be here. I have a horrible feeling that Scarlett knows Grace and my history.

So. This is practically an ambush.

Fucking hell.

"How can you two *possibly* know each other?" King asks again. "There's no way you've met already."

Then Grace speaks.

"Duke and I go way back, don't we, Duke?"

"You're Scarlett's flatmate?" I ask her.

"And *best friend*," Scarlett replies.

"King said I should meet you. He said I would like you and that you will like me."

"Did he? Well, he was wrong."

Silence falls in the room.

Grace continues to stare at me like she wants to kill me. Scarlett stands there, supportive of her best friend. I grip my Scotch glass tightly and try to remain composed.

King just looks incredibly confused by the whole situation.

"I need to talk to you," I say to Grace, breaking the tension.

She's like a gust of wind. I want to catch her before she disappears out of my life again for another four years.

She gives me a look of pure disgust.

Shit. Talking to this girl is gonna be a lot harder than I thought.

"You don't *need* anything from me," she replies without a note of emotion. "I *want* nothing to do with you. Ever. I can't believe I'm even in the same bloody room as you."

King still looks confused.

"Sweetheart," I say. "You wouldn't come all this way across town to tell me you want nothing to do with me. I know you want to talk. We *have* to talk about what happened."

Grace crosses her arms.

"Nope."

"Then why are you here?"

"To look after my best friend. Is that a problem?"

"Well, I certainly didn't wake up this morning expecting this to happen today," I say quietly. "You really are a blast from the past, Grace, and I certainly would love to have a word with you in private. Let's go over a few things."

"I would love to punch you in your smug face, but we can't have everything we want."

Scarlett, sensing the tension in the air, steps in between us as if Grace and I are about to come to blows. "I think we should go, Grace."

"Make sure you two stay safe," King blurts out, still completely flummoxed by what the hell's happening. "Message me, Scarlett."

Truth be told, so am I.

"We will."

Grace continues to shoot daggers in my direction.

"You're clearly in no state to talk to me at the present time," I say to the girl. "You seem pretty angry."

"You've got that right."

"I think you should go with your flatmate," I continue. "But we will talk, Grace. If not now, then another time."

She doesn't budge. "No, we won't. Never."

I smile. She came here to make this dramatic announcement. She came to this penthouse to really surprise me. Well, it worked. I didn't know she was Scarlett's flatmate. Unlike her, I didn't know we had a connection, so if she really didn't want to see me, then she wouldn't have come.

Oh, she wants me.

She and I will definitely talk, I am sure of it. Now that I know who she is, there's no escaping.

I want to find out *exactly* what happened four years ago. I want to hear her explanation for why she disappeared that morning.

Scarlett takes her friend by the shoulder and guides her out the front door as I watch.

Grace's eyes stay with me until the door shuts. Her eyes burn into me.

Oh, darling.

We. Will. Talk.

14

GRACE

The Tube shuffles along the dark tunnel, and I sit there thinking about what the fuck's just happened inside King's penthouse.

Sitting next to me, Scarlett reaches over and takes my hand in hers, squeezing tight in a sisterly display of affection. I turn to look at her, smiling weakly.

"You okay?" she asks me in her cute American accent.

"Yep."

"It must've been pretty weird seeing Duke again."

"Yep. It definitely was."

We come to a stop at a station. A few people come on the train.

No matter how crazy the last few hours have been, at least I have my best friend beside me through all of this. One good silver lining.

But that still does not mean Duke's presence does not rattle me to the core.

He was right there... in the same room as me.

Seeing that man brought back so many memories I had buried. Those few days of thrill and excitement.

The *cockiness* of Duke as I told him I wanted nothing to do with him has shaken me. The casual confidence he still oozed, even after being surprised by me in the penthouse. And his fucking charming smirk that could melt the panties off any girl still rattled me. God, his arrogance was so annoying to witness.

Cheating bastard.

How did I manage to eat it all up four years ago?

Oh. Right. I was an innocent eighteen-year-old barely adult woman desperate for the attention of an effortlessly charming man. I was easy prey.

But, back at King's penthouse, he was also so dominating. That's something I'd nearly forgotten about him. Even when I strolled in dramatically to try to shock him, he still remained his cool composure. So effing tall and muscular and dressed so goddamn sharply in a tailored suit. A perfect display of masculine power. Seeing the gorgeous man standing there in his brother's luxury flat with that tumbler glass raised to his full wet lips made my pussy throb with longing.

That's why I ate him up all those years ago. That's why I still want to wrap my legs around his broad frame and consume him, even though I hate him with every fiber of my being.

I don't know whether I want to punch him or kiss him. Jesus, my head is so messed up right now.

He must know why I walked out that day four years ago, right?

The man was - *and maybe still is* - married. With kids. No way was I going to be some pining mistress.

I want him to hurt. To feel the guilt of being a cheater. To know how inexcusable his actions were.

"What exactly happened between you two?" Scarlett asks me as the Tube stops at Charing Cross. I watch the doors squeak open and close before I answer.

"I found out the morning after we slept together that he's married."

"Oh," Scarlett replies, her mouth open. "Wow. That sucks."

"Yeah, it really does."

She's starting to see a new side to me. A side I've kept hidden from others. Sure, I've been on a lot of dates the last few years. I've had a lot of fun running around Soho. I've met so many people. I'm a loud, gregarious person.

But the truth is that there's a reason I'm so extroverted. I'm trying to hide something. Underneath my shiny veneer of a fun-loving, carefree woman is a scared young girl trying to nurse a broken heart.

I just don't ever want to make myself as vulnerable again as that awful morning I left Duke's penthouse four years ago. I will never let myself be used like that again. I cried for days.

And I built up a persona. I made myself into Grace Madden. The party girl with friends all around this never-sleeping city.

It's an armor. And now, with the knowledge that Duke is King's brother, I feel like that once-impenetrable armor is being chipped away.

I'm scared again. My heart is once again exposed. Will Duke get to me again?

I thought I was strong, but one look at the man and I'm back to being that broken-hearted young girl again.

One of the new passengers on our train is a mother with a newborn. She sits down opposite us, keeping a hold of the pram. The baby looks so tiny. So incredibly cute. The mother takes the sleepy child out of her pram and holds her against her chest. The baby gurgles and opens its eyes towards us. Its big soft cheeks are pink.

"Adorable," I whisper. The mother smiles back at me and Scarlett squeezes my hand. She agrees.

The baby giggles at us. Scarlett and I wave back.

"I didn't know Duke's married," Scarlett mutters. "But, then again, I don't know that much about King's older brother."

"I think he keeps his cards pretty close to the chest. I bet he has had a lot of side-chicks in the last four years. I wouldn't put it past him. He's nothing but a liar and a predator."

"God, his poor wife."

"Yep. And he has kids, which made the whole affair even more sordid. I got out of his apartment as quickly as I could when I found out."

Scarlett turns to me, gob smacked. "Wow. He's really got a double life, doesn't he? I didn't know King was an uncle."

"I guess the Heath-Harding boys keep a lot of secrets."

"King would never hide anything from me. I just haven't asked about kids before."

"Maybe Duke's marriage fell apart," I suggest. "I mean, it was four years ago since I've last seen him. Maybe he's abandoned his family. I wouldn't be surprised with nothing less from a cheating asshole."

"He may be a cheater, but he *is* King's brother," Scarlett says.

I feel sorry for her. She's trying so hard to justify the actions of her lovely boyfriend's bad older brother.

"I mean nothing against King. That man is nothing but a saint in my eyes," I reply. "But there's always a black sheep in the family, and I think Duke fits that role pretty perfectly if that night four years ago is anything to go on."

"How did you know he was married?"

"There were photos in his apartment. Lots of photos. He with a bride on their wedding day. Him with two kids."

"Oh, Grace. I am so sorry."

"Don't worry," I reply, flicking my hair back like I'm throwing away the memory of Duke. "I've moved past him since. I'm my own woman now. I don't need the attention of a man whore to feel good about myself."

The Tube train continues to trundle along the tunnel to our stop. We wave one last time to the baby. It giggles again. The mother winks at us.

"Your baby is so cute," I say.

"She keeps me up all night," the mom responds. "I don't when it was the last time I slept, but she is worth it."

Scarlett and I both stand up, reaching for the railing as the train comes to a halt. Scarlett wraps her arm around me and rests her head on my shoulder as we wait for the doors to open. I inhale her sweet perfume and smile softly to myself.

I'm so glad we've found each other.

"So, what you said at King's place is true, then?" Scarlett asks me, her voice muffled against my boobs. "You want nothing at all to do with Duke?"

"Scarlett, I never want to see the man again."

But, as we step off the train onto the station platform, there's a dark feeling growing in the pit of my stomach.

I just know that I'm going to be seeing Duke again.

15

DUKE

Oʜ, I am *definitely* going to see Grace again.

Despite her protestations to the contrary, she and I are gonna talk.

She's the girl that got away, and no girl has ever done that to me. I need to converse with her. The girl that disappeared - the girl I've spent four years secretly searching for – there's no way I'm letting her slip through my fingers once again.

She's fallen right into my lap, and she apparently wants *nothing* to do with me. That was her words.

Well, we'll see about that.

"You know that girl?" I ask King the moment Scarlett and Grace walk out his front door.

"I was going to ask you the exact same thing, Duke. What the hell just happened? What the fuck was that weird tension between you two?"

Oh. Right. My brother is incredibly confused. He looks at me with complete bewilderment.

"Have I not told you about her?"

"You never tell me anything, Duke. You're always a closed book, especially with women."

Well, he's right there.

I never speak to others about my love life, even my brother. I prefer matters of the heart to be kept close to my chest. Never brag. Never tell. Never show any sign of vulnerability.

I don't need to confide in anyone.

I take in a long breath and refill my Scotch glass. I'm going to need alcohol to get through this confession to my sibling.

"She and I had a thing about four years back," I say.

My brother eyes me suspiciously.

"A *thing*?"

"Sex, King. A one-night stand. Do you need me to explain the birds and the bees to you?"

He rolls his eyes.

"Of course. But you've had so many girls over the years that I thought you might've lost count."

I take a long sip of my Scotch.

"That I have."

"And you remember this one girl, this same girl who's turned out, miraculously, to be Scarlett's flatmate?"

"Yes."

"Wow."

I absentmindedly swivel the alcohol around in the glass and stare off into the distance. "It seems like the universe has brought us back together," I add quietly.

"I've never heard you be so damn philosophical," King says. "So, what makes Grace special?"

Okay, I'm *really* going to need alcohol to get me through this.

I take in a deep breath and continue. I might as well tell my brother now. It's too late to stop.

"She's the one girl I can't stop thinking about, King. Ever since that night with her... I just can't explain. It's like tasting the sweetest and richest chocolate in the world and then never being allowed to touch it again. From then on, no other chocolate can ever dare compare to that first bite; you simply have to taste that original again. You might spend the rest of your life chasing after a phantom in the hope of tasting that first one again. This is... *something* like that. Grace has been that phantom for me. The sweetest and richest bar of chocolate."

King shakes his head.

"Wow, Duke. I've never seen you tongue-tied over a woman before."

"Shut up, prick."

"She's really affected you, huh?"

Another gulp of Scotch.

"You could say that."

King laughs and shakes his head. He sits down on his couch and leans back, staring at me in confusion the entire time.

"This is crazier than I thought," he says. "I need a moment to process this. My brother the love-stricken fool. You can't make this shit up."

"Take all the time you need. I'm still processing seeing the damn girl's face for the first time in forever."

King smiles cheekily at me. Any other situation and I would gladly wipe that smirk off his face with a playful jab, but right now I'm still in shock. I don't have the energy to rebuke my brother.

"She's really rocked you to your core, hasn't she?" he asks me.

"That's one way of putting it," I reply.

"But you're *Duke Heath-Harding*," my brother continues. "You're famous for having a heart even colder than mine. How has this even possibly happened?"

"I guess Grace has been the one girl in the entire world who's managed to melt my cold heart. That's why I want to see her again. That's why I was so fucking thrown a minute ago when she walked through your door."

"Damn."

I take another swig of the fiery Scotch.

"Yep. Damn."

I look down at my hand. It's shaking with excitement. I'm so affected by Grace's appearance.

That has never happened before.

I have never been so nervous or thrilled at seeing someone in my life.

King whistles in amazement.

"Well, Grace is a firecracker, that's for sure."

"She certainly is."

"She's not going to give in without a fight. *That* was pretty clear just then. That look in her eyes..."

"She definitely isn't."

"Even to you with all your charm and looks. It's going to be one hell of a fight."

"Oh, I know."

"So, Duke. What are you going to do?"

I glance up and lock eyes with my brother. I'm being deadly serious.

"I am going to do what every Heath-Harding boy does when faced with a challenge. I am not going to rest until I get my prize."

16

GRACE

DUKE IS STANDING in my bedroom. At my open doorway. Waiting for me to wake up.

"Duke?" I ask, blinking my eyes open. "What are you doing here?"

I'm frozen in shock.

He's actually standing in *my bedroom*, and I am totally naked under my bedsheets.

I gulp.

"What are you doing in my room?" I ask him again, trepidation filling my words.

"I'm here for you, Grace," he says softly as he closes my bedroom door behind him, locking us both in here alone.

I don't move.

"You're... in my bedroom..."

"I know that," he replies in a whisper. "I'm here to claim what is mine. I'm here to take what's been withdrawn from me for years. *You.*"

My mouth drops open.

"You can't have me," I retort.

My voice is wavering. Unsure.

Duke takes a step towards my bed. He looks at me with an impenetrable and single-minded stare. I know he can't be stopped. I lick my dry lips. I am both terrified and turned on by the presence of this man in my most private space.

"You're trespassing," I mutter. "This is insane. You know you'll be sent to jail for this, right?"

I don't know how he's managed to get in here into my flat, but at the same time, I'm not complaining. There's a sick part of me that *wants* him here alone with me. In some deep and twisted part of me, I want him to claim me as his.

"I can have whatever I want," Duke says. "You may try to fight, but I know you'll give in to me, Grace. You *know* you want to give into me."

Oh, that I do know.

There's no battling him now. All my defenses ebb away as the man takes more steps towards m, lying naked in my bed until he's standing right above me. I can feel his hot breath on my exposed skin. There is only a thin bedsheet separating my bare body from his sight.

And, my God, I am incredibly wet.

"You're a monster," I say as he starts to slowly peel back the bedsheet. I make no effort to stop him.

"And you're my willing prey," he replies. "If you really hate me so much, why haven't you screamed yet?"

"I will. Don't try me."

He leans down so that his lips brush my ear. I'm shaking in aroused terror.

"I'll give you a reason to scream... in *pleasure*."

I gulp again. I have no words.

He rips the bedsheet away from my naked body and I

look up at him in wonder. He grins at me. The exact same grin he had when he'd tied me up four years ago. That grin that makes my heart flutter.

This man truly is a monster, and I'm going to let him devour me.

Duke removes his shirt with one sexy pull over his head. I glance down his muscular torso. He's absolutely dripping in sweat. There's a distinct bulge in his pants. Oh, I remember that massive cock.

"I'm going to fuck you, Grace. I'm going to fuck you in that pretty mouth of yours."

I don't object.

Instead, I open my mouth wide as Duke yanks down his pants and his member bolts out in front of my face.

Jesus, it's so veiny and swollen. I must taste it.

Without waiting for a command, I take him in between my greedy lips. Duke groans in a frenzy of passion as my wetness engulfs him. His excitement turns me on even more, and I shudder in delight.

"I'm claiming what's mine," he whispers breathlessly. "You should never have dared to resist me in the first place. You know you belong to me."

I know this is wrong. I know he should not be in here. I know I should be angry at him for tricking me as he did.

But, God, the man is so incredibly sexy. I simply can't help myself.

"I want you to drink me in, Grace. I want to fill you up."

Boy, he can do whatever he wants with me.

His strong hands grip the back of my neck, and he pushes in deeper. I can sense that he's about to cum.

Duke moans as his juice floods into my mouth. I inhale it zealously. He's so salty. So *manly*.

"You're all mine now," he says as the last splurges of cum drip onto my eager tongue. My mouth is full of him.

He's right. Damn, he's so right.

* * *

I WAKE up from my dream sweating and breathing heavily.

I look around my bedroom. Duke isn't here.

He never was here.

It was just a dream. It was just a dream. It was just a dream.

I tell myself that over and over, and yet I can't shake the feeling that the dream was just so bloody real. I rip off my bedsheets and look down at my naked body.

Oh my god, I orgasmed from a dream. I feel so dirty.

Grace...

And, somehow, it turns me on even more. My body feels like it's on fire. I've not experienced a thrill like this for a very long time.

I take a moment to calm myself. My breathing falls under control. My rapidly rising chest slows down. I close my eyes and cool down. I lean back against my pillow and sigh.

My head is consumed with thoughts of Duke Heath-Harding, and it disgusts me.

I think about waking Scarlett to tell her about this – to talk through my crazy mind – but I don't want to disturb her. It's the middle of the night.

I slowly get out of bed and stagger into the kitchen naked – too lazy to dress – to get myself a glass of much-needed water. I swig it down and pat the sweat from off my forehead with the back of my hand.

I need to get Duke out of my head somehow. Even my flipping dreams are full of him.

I hate him so much for what he did to me, but I hate him even more for how he makes me feel.

I put the empty glass in the kitchen sink and limp back into my bedroom.

It was so bad of me to see Duke today. I gave in to temptation. Why was I so damn curious?

Grace, what have you gotten yourself into?

17

GRACE

THE OFFICE for the tour guide company I work for is extremely small, even for London standards. I take a step inside. Harsh fluorescent light greets me. I blink.

It's less an office space and more a place for us tour guides to simply dump our stuff. Essentially, a pigsty. There's a large table in the middle covered with used food wrappers and discarded water bottles. There are two computers that are from the early noughties plugged into the wall for us to work from. The whole tour guide operation runs from Windows Ninety-Eight.

Definitely do not check out our antiquated monstrosity of a website, that's all I can say.

This company is in dire need of being bought by someone who knows what they're doing. Tour guides in London is a booming business, but this company seems determined to remain in the dark ages.

I head straight for my tiny locker and violently push my bag inside, picking up my tour guide badge and taking a seat at the table. I find the things I'm going to need for my tour. The clipboard with my group's names on it. A pen. A torch.

I've done this job so many times that it's second nature to me. I love it, though. Really *bloody* love it.

I pull out a battered sandwich I made a home and unwrap the clingfilm from around it.

There's only one other person in the room. Another tour guide called Antony. He's middle-aged. He pretends he's into fitness and boxing - he absolutely *loves* bragging about how often he does it - but he's got a little belly poking out under his shirt and no upper body definition at all, which is all you need to know about what kind of guy he is. His misplaced self-righteousness can be a real turnoff. I usually try to avoid him. His "banter" can really be rough and inappropriate.

At the end of last year, he went on "holiday" for a few weeks in Turkey and came back to work with a noticeably thicker head of hair and a pulled-forward hairline. Clearly the work of some backstreet doctor over there. His mouth can run off with the most ridiculous stories that he all assets are true. Some of the other women at the tour company have alerted me to the fact that he has a history of being a bit of a creep around girls, which explains why he once tried to fill me up with multiple vodka shots one time at the pub.

Let's just say that Tony is not my favorite person to work with.

And now he's sitting opposite me with his legs wide apart, dominating the space, a newspaper open between his hands.

His eyes poke above the top of the paper, observing me as I quietly eat my sandwich.

"You heard that we might be under new management?" Tony asks me eventually.

"What?"

"There was an email today about it."

Oh, shit.

"New management? I didn't get any email," I say. "Does it change anything for us?"

"Not much. I think it's just a new owner of the place. I don't think they'll want to overhaul everything."

"How can you know that?"

Antony sniffs and dramatically taps his forehead with a finger. "I just know these things. I've got *intuition*. I'm pretty street-smart."

"Right," I reply. I just want to get back to my sandwich, but this new information is certainly intriguing. Enough for me to continue to chat with Antony. "Do you think we'll have to close?"

"Nope. They say they want to continue the operation."

"Oh, good," I reply.

"I guess we'll have to wait to see what happens."

"Yeah, I guess so too."

"Besides, I'm too good a tour guide to be the first to go if there are any cuts. I'm on top of the board here."

He's lying. He's around the fourth-best tour guide here. Out of five.

"Have you read about this whole murder investigation?" Antony asks, nodding down at the page in the newspaper he's reading. "Shocking stuff."

He's talking about King and Ben and the Prestige.

"Yeah, it's gruesome," I reply. My tour doesn't start for another half hour, which is why I'm sitting here. I thought it'll just be me in the office today – I'm the only one who's put down on the schedule - but it seems like Tony has decided to make himself at home.

"Didn't you say your flatmate was involved in all of this?" he asks, staring at me with one eyebrow raised.

I had made the silly mistake of telling people the other

day, before the threat on King's life, that it was someone at Scarlett's work that was murdered. I wanted to sound interesting at work to my friend, alright? I didn't realize how serious it all really was.

But Tony must've overheard it.

"Uh, yeah. It happened at her work."

"Wow," Tony whistles annoyingly and tuts loudly. "Imagine that. Someone murdering you at work. Sounds like one of the tours we give."

"Yep."

Our company specializes in historical serial killer tours of London. Yeah, I know. How very *cliche* of me. I spend all my time at home watching true crime documentaries and then I spend all my time at work recounting them to tourists.

But I do love this job.

It isn't the best paid, but the shocked and awed expressions on people's faces as I reveal to them that they're standing exactly on a site where, two hundred years ago, some poor prostitute was killed is worth every penny. I love showing people a good time, and I'm passionate about true crime. So, here we are.

I mean, it's much better than working at Small.

"How about this billionaire bloke getting threatened by the killer? That's pretty cool."

Tony is now talking about King. He doesn't know the extent of the connection between me and the *billionaire bloke*. I'll like to very much keep it that way.

"Must be horrible having a threat made against your life like that," I reply.

"Hm," Tony purses his lips together, lowering the newspaper to look me directly in the eye. "But imagine being that killer, though. You're famous now. Imagine killing a Heath-Harding boy. That would surely make your name live in infamy forever, won't it? They'd make films of you. Heck, they might even give a tour about you in a hundred years. That's certainly a way to leave your mark on the world. The killer could even get rich writing a book about it from jail."

I hate the casual way Tony is talking about this. Someone has died, and he's busy thinking about how to make money from it.

"I dunno," I say, rising up from my chair and throwing my rubbish in the bin. "Sounds like just another prick trying to get in the paper."

As I pass him, Tony suddenly reaches out and grabs my wrist. "I imagine this Kingsley guy is next. What do you think?"

He leisurely looks my body up and down. Taking me in like I'm a piece of candy.

Is he being turned on by this?

I quickly yank my wrist away from him.

"I think I better get to work, Tony. And so should you."

I immediately head for the office door and step outside, not wanting to linger near that man any longer.

The other girls at work are so right. Tony *is* a creep.

I shake off the uncomfortable thought of him eyeballing my body up and down and head towards the Tube station where my tour is set to start.

I usually wait outside the station just before the beginning of the tour. It's where the booking says for my group to meet. I register everyone off the booking clipboard that I've taken from the office, making sure they've all paid for the tour.

It's getting towards seven in the evening. The sun is slowly going down.

Today is a pretty busy group. I like that. A big crowd means big reactions. Unlike the usual London weather, it's not supposed to rain tonight. Yep, I can't wait to start.

"Okay, everyone. We're just about to begin. Get in close."

I gather the group around me. I check my clipboard. There's only one other person to join. I scan across the column to their name.

I didn't read it before.

My heart immediately drops when I see the name.

Oh no.

Of course.

Duke's booked the tour.

Of course he bloody has.

The bastard.

A shadow falls across the clipboard as I stare, shocked, at his name. I look up.

And there he is. As if summoned by dark supernatural forces the moment I read his name. A tall, handsome shadow standing over me. He's here.

I just *knew* I would see him again.

Memories of that sex dream the other night come flooding back.

Not now, Grace. Don't think of him that way.

It's so hard not to.

And then he speaks.

"I believe I'm booked in, Miss Madden."

Fuck.

My body shivers at the sight of him. I'm drawn to his lips that are curled in that charming smirk of his. I remember the forceful taste of those lips on mine. How I melted under his touch.

And now he's here, and he's about to join my tour.

18

GRACE

"So, let's start the tour," I say, gesturing to the group to gather around me. We'd passed the station and were on our first stop on the walk tonight. This is where I make the introductions. Set the scene. I always love this part. "First, I want to take you back to nineteenth-century London. A time of mist and fog. Where you can get drunk for only a few stolen shillings, where you can hire an ugly disease-ridden prostitute for nothing more than the promise of a shot of gin, where murderers shrouded in dark cloaks lurk on every street corner..."

"Show us a murder, then. Hurry up."

Everyone's head whips around to the back of the group where Duke stands formidably with his arms crossed and that trademark smirk on his face. Being so tall and broad-shouldered, he's incredibly imposing and attention-grabbing. Especially how he rises up behind everyone. You just *have* to look at him. The charisma shines off him like he's the fucking sun. Most of the women in my audience – young and old – swoon at him.

Bloody hell.

I had no choice but to let the man join the tour; he has *bought* a ticket. I have told him twice to get off my tour. To go home. And twice he blanked me.

And now he's just interrupted me. Of course he has.

I give him an evil eye.

Get the hint, twat.

I choose to ignore him and continue talking, my group's attention slowly drifting back to me. I put in all my effort at a serious and somber tone to offset the asshole standing at the back.

Blank the bastard, Grace.

"What you're about to hear on this tour is not for the faint-hearted. There are gruesome killings involved and sad stories about women who, through no fault of their own, had to work on the streets for scraps..."

"Get on with it."

Ignore him. Ignore him. Ignore him.

I will ignore him like he's a little naughty schoolboy. He's only going to feed off my frustration. I can't give him the satisfaction of getting visibly annoyed.

"Let's head now, down this alley, to our first murder site."

"Finally."

Ugh. What have I done to deserve this?

The group follows me like eager ducklings as we cross the street and into the alley with me keeping a watchful eye on Duke. He trails behind the group, only staring at me.

Why is he here? Why does he want to annoy me so much?

I want him gone, but I'd be wrong to not admit that his sudden appearance on my tour thrills me. It's the danger. It's the sheer wrongness of him chasing me like this. He simply does not give a fuck about what others think of him.

But he should not be here. He should be at home. With his family. The same people he *cheated* on when he brought me back to his apartment four years ago.

The tourists love this alley, that's why I use it to properly start my tour. It really takes them back to their imagined fantasy of Victorian England.

"Okay, everyone," I say, my voice reverberating around the alley and my captive audience. "I want you to all close your eyes."

I stare right on back at Duke. He winks at me slyly before following my order.

"Good. Now I want you to take yourself back to that time I've just mentioned, the time full of rogues and inept police. A time where you had to fight to survive on the mean streets of London. I want you to imagine yourself as a drunk and destitute prostitute, staggering down this alleyway so late at night that it's early morning. I want you to feel eyes upon you. There's a man at one end of this alleyway in a top hat and cloak, and he's got something shining in his hand. Is it a blade? What would you do?"

Everyone murmurs in fear, all their eyes tightly closed. This bit of my tour is always like a strange sort of hypnotism, where they'll happily stay in this trance and imagine the terrors.

I usually love to revel in the atmosphere, but not tonight.

"Take a moment to absorb your surroundings..."

I leave them and dart around to the back of the group.

Where Duke is, his eyes also shut.

I whisper into his ear so that no one else can hear, but I make it venomous enough to show him I'm not afraid of him.

"What the hell are you doing here?"

The man doesn't seem shocked by my voice appearing suddenly by his side. He smiles again as soon as I speak, like he has been expecting me to talk to him.

So fucking cheeky.

"I could ask you the same thing," he whispers. "I could ask you what you're doing still working. You do know there's a murderer about, right?"

Then he blinks open his blue eyes. He turns to me with the calmness of a man who's easily won every battle he's ever fought in life.

Well, I'm certainly going to put up a fight.

"I can take perfectly good care of myself, thank you very much."

"You sure you don't need protection?"

"Nope."

"I can help you," he replies. "You sure you don't feel scared about this killer on the loose? I can be there for you, Grace."

"I don't know how many times I can stress this," I say. "But I'm going to repeat myself. Get. Off. My. Tour."

Duke reaches out and takes my chin between his fingers. Just like he did back at Small all those years ago. His touch quickens my breathing and sends pangs of pleasure down to my core.

I hate him - *I really fucking do* - but his presence does things to my body I can't deny. The way he's pursuing me. How he isn't giving up. It all turns me on, and it makes me so effing infuriated.

But I'm no cheater, and I certainly am not going to help Duke cheat.

"Get off my tour," I repeat again, louder this time, as I pull my face free from his grasp.

"Don't you mean *my* tour?" he asks me.

"What?"

"*My* tour."

"What the hell are you talking about, Duke?"

"Haven't you heard, Grace?" His blue eyes sparkle at me like he's won a competition I didn't know we're participating in. "I've bought the tour company. You're my employee now."

What. The. Fuck?

I just glare at the man, wishing so very hard to slap him on his perfect face right now.

But I'm in the middle of work. I can't exactly commit an act of violence in front of all these tourists. Even with their eyes closed.

"You're lying."

"I'm not. Check your email. See who pays you. It's my company now."

"You can piss right off."

"Come on, Grace. I've paid for my ticket. I'm enjoying hearing *all* about Victorian England."

I just can't win, can't I?

"Don't you dare interrupt the rest of the tour," I venomously threaten him.

He remains completely composed, like he's rehearsed this all already.

"I need something in return in order to do that, Grace. This is my tour company, after all. You can't do shit to get rid of me."

I cross my arms and take a step back from the man.

"What do you want, Duke? What can I do to stop you from interrupting my work?"

"I want to chat to you about what happened four years ago."

"You bought an entire company just so you can talk to me?"

He smiles.

"Something like that."

"Don't you dare ruin this job. I *love* this job, Duke. It's the one thing that keeps me sane."

"I'm not going to do anything with it, I promise. I simply bought it so I can speak to you this evening."

What kind of level is this man on? He's bought a whole company just to have a conversation?

"Promises from you mean nothing," I reply. "Don't interrupt me again."

"How about you talk to me, and I won't interrupt the tour? That's something you can trust."

I guess he's finally got me. I have to speak to him now.

"Okay. Fine. I will talk to you after we're finished, but only if you don't utter another single word from your stupid mouth for the next hour. Understood?"

"Crystal clear, Miss Grace."

I grunt and return to the front of the tour group, feeling Duke's eyes burn into the back of me.

Even in public, with all these people around, he has an air of danger about him. This man who, at the snap of his fingers, can get anything he desires. What could he do to me? What could he take from me?

Everything. That's what.

He has the money. The prestige.

The power.

I continue with the tour. We head to all the murder sites of Jack the Ripper. I keep my audience enthralled with tales of murder and violence. They eat it all up, as usual.

I don't want to brag, but even with the shadow of Duke lurking around, I am still so fucking *good* at my job.

I really do love it.

And then we end the tour in front of St Paul's Cathedral. A massive white dome-shaped place of worship right in the center of London. This is one of my favorite places in the whole of the city, and I tell my tour group exactly that.

I stand awkwardly as they all applaud me and hand me bundles of tips. I make good money from this job. I don't even want to think about Duke buying the company. I really don't want to lose this thing I've got going for me. It's the one thing I'm good at.

Duke himself lingers until every audience member has thanked me and moved on, his presence like a looming apocalypse. He actually kept to his word. Nothing squeaked past his gorgeous lips the entire tour.

Great. I'm gonna have to talk to this guy now.

"What do you want?" he asks me when everyone has gone and it's just us two standing on the steps of the Cathedral.

"What?"

"What do you want right now, Grace?"

I shrug. "You're really leading with that question? I just want to help Scarlett. Keep her safe and find whoever threatened Kingsley."

Duke nods. "Then you should work with me."

I scoff loudly. "How about *no*? Why would I want to work with you?"

"You're smart, Grace," Duke says. "And I've got all the resources in the world. It's simple. How about we work together?"

"Not after the way you treated me four years ago, Duke. Not with that behavior."

"Look, I can give you money."

And that makes my blood boil.

"Money? Do you think I can be bought? You're such an asshole, Duke."

That's the final straw. I've had it with these rich men with their bountiful pockets thinking they can just stomp all over the place with no care for anyone just because they can buy you off.

I am not motivated by money. Nothing in my life is motivated by money.

And I certainly don't need Duke's.

"Grace..."

He starts, but I don't let him finish.

"Just take your money and piss off, Duke. I don't care anymore. I don't care about you buying my company, you can have it. Get out of my life. Just. Piss. Off."

And then I turn and run up the stairs. I want to get away from this man, and the only place I can go is inside St Paul's Cathedral.

And Duke follows me inside.

19

DUKE

She doesn't stop, even when I call her name.

"Grace. *Grace.*"

She continues inside St Paul's Cathedral, and I chase behind, wishing her to stop.

"Grace."

The Cathedral is one of the most iconic sights in the whole of London. It's a massive building. Inside, it stretches on forever, and the ceiling is so incredibly high up. You're instantly presented with an expanse so big it just takes your breath away.

If Grace is awed by the design of the building, it doesn't register in her behavior. She continues to march away from me, her arms folded around her like a defensive shield.

And I continue to follow.

I'm catching up to her now as she races down the aisle of the Cathedral. She's no match for my long athletic legs, strengthened from years of rugby training and gym sessions.

I can almost reach out and touch her now; I'm that close.

"Grace."

"Shush." A passing priest raises his finger to his lips and glares at me.

"Sorry," I whisper, but I don't mean it.

The robed man's intervention causes Grace to spin around to face me. She smiles.

"You better be quiet, Duke," she says, her voice low. "You gotta whisper in here."

Oh, she's a viper, alright. Ready to strike at me.

I like the bite on her. The fight in her eyes.

It only makes me want her more.

Right now, I've got to apologize for what I said outside the Cathedral. I know I have to start with that to even get Grace's attention.

"That was a bad way to phrase it, I'll admit," I say to her, trying my hardest to keep my voice at a whisper. "I didn't mean that I'll throw money at you, just that I want to help my brother and your flatmate. I think you and I should work together in stopping this killer before he wrecks even more havoc."

The priest continues to glare at me from across the aisle like I'm the devil. Well, I'm sure there are plenty of girls that would agree with his assessment of me.

I ignore him.

Grace keeps her arms folded tight to her chest. She purses her sweet lips and narrows her eyes at me.

"You really want me to help you?" she asks.

"Yep."

"Why should I? After what you did four years ago, I should never speak to you again."

Now it's my time to bite back.

"Why are you making out that it was all my fault? You're the one that vanished into thin air."

She rolls her eyes at me.

"I don't want to get into this with you, Duke. Go. Away."

"Why did you disappear?" I ask. "Everything seemed to be going well, and then you just *evaporated*. You even left your dress in my room, and I couldn't find you. I came out of the shower to find you gone. *Puff*. What the hell happened?"

Grace juts her head forward towards me aggressively. Man, how I wish I could just take her face between my hands and kiss her into submission.

"I have no need to explain," she replies.

"What does that mean?" I ask just as the priest returns with a vengeance, hushing me loudly.

I turn to him and stare back with ice in my eyes until he backs away.

Even a man of God can't tell me what to do.

"I'm really not having this conversation," Grace whispers, shaking her head. "I've told you enough times that what you did was *so* wrong."

"Don't you realize I've spent four years looking for you?" I'm not paying attention to the priest's indignant looks. Grace is far more important than keeping my voice down. "You blocked me on social media. I couldn't find you at all. You were like a ghost, and I honestly don't get it when that night we spent together was one of the best nights of my life. Surely, it must've been the same for you."

"It was," she replies.

"Then why did you go?"

Grace scoffs like I'm stupid.

I don't know why she's acting like this. Putting up these walls. It's making me insane, and I never go crazy over a girl.

Why does she think I was an asshole?

My cock twitches. I've never had such pushback from a girl in my life. Grace is definitely the one I remember out of the dozens I've been with. The one girl I can't get out of my head.

"That one-night stand with you has ruined sex for me forever," I tell her. Yeah, I'm talking about sex while in a cathedral, but I'm sure God will let me off this one. I'm sure He also wants to know why she left me. "I've been looking for you ever since that morning. You know that, don't you?"

"I don't care," she retorts.

"Grace, I even went to that shop you worked at, and the boss told me you'd quit. I looked *everywhere* for you – all over this fucking city - but I couldn't find you. I have to know why you went. It's been driving me insane like you wouldn't believe. I *have* to know."

"Look at you," Grace replies with a smirk. "The *great* Duke Heath-Harding – king of his domain - not knowing what he's done wrong. It's pretty pathetic."

My voice lowers.

"Tell me why you left, Grace."

"If I even have to explain to you why I went, then you're even more of an idiot than I thought you were."

And with that, Grace turns and heads to a side exit of the Cathedral.

I growl and rush to her, stopping her by the door.

"What can I do?" I ask her. "What can I say to make you explain?"

Jesus, it's like I'm begging.

Grace scowls back at me.

"An apology is a good start, don't you think?"

"Sweetheart, if there's one thing you got to know about me is that I'm not apologizing for anything."

20

GRACE

So.

He's now saying that he has nothing to apologize for? *Nothing* at all?

Is he freaking blind and stupid?

That crosses the line. It makes me see red. I immediately tear away from Duke and head into the side room of St Paul's, where there are stairs that lead all the way up into the roof's dome.

And, as always, he follows me. Up the entire staircase.

This time he doesn't call my name. He just stalks me silently, like a bad dream. I don't give him the satisfaction of looking behind at him.

I don't even know where I'm going, just as long as I'm getting away from him. I need some fresh air, and I find it upstairs.

The staircase leads onto the balcony that rings the outside of St Paul's dome. The wind nearly knocks me back as I step out onto the terrace, but I steady myself on the railing. We're so high up and so exposed to the elements.

The view of London that greets me is breathtaking. I look out over the river and the West End. I can see all the places I take my tour groups to. The lights of Piccadilly Circus in the distance. The Strand opened up below like an airport runway.

It's the city I love.

The door swings open behind me and Duke steps out. He doesn't care at all about the view, only about me. I sense his focus on me like a laser beam.

I keep my back to him even when he walks up and stands beside me by the balcony's railings, looking out over the Thames. I feel his arm brush against mine.

Oh, I'm still angry.

He takes in a long breath, and I roll my eyes, preferring to keep my attention away from him and on London.

"You know, I have been unable to play my saxophone since that night," he says softly.

Now that makes me laugh.

That came out of nowhere.

"Come on, big boy, stop being such a child," I reply through my snorts of derision. "I literally do *not* care. Can't you see that?"

"Why are you being so heartless?" he asks.

And that's when I feel pure rage bubble up inside me. Anger. Fury that comes from deep in my bones.

How thick can this guy be?

"Maybe it's because when I see you, all I think of is your wife. Those two kids you have. Maybe *they* might be the reason why I'm so heartless, you cheater."

It finally all comes out.

"Ah."

Everything goes quiet between us. Duke turns his

head to look out over London and I grip the railing, debating whether to just end this stupid conversation and head back down the stairs or stay here in Duke's awkward silence.

"I guess I need to explain that," he says softly.

You think?

"I guess you do. You can't just fuck a girl behind your wife's back and expect everything to be all *hunky-dory*."

Duke nods. His energy remains calm, and it makes me even more infuriated. He doesn't seem to understand the gravity of this conversation.

"I guess I really have to explain some things."

"*Bingo.*"

"Follow me," he says.

"What?"

"Follow me."

I shake my head. "No way am I doing that."

Then Duke actually *sighs* like I'm being unreasonable and offers out his hand towards me. "Follow me downstairs. I've got to show you something."

"I'm not doing anything with you."

"Come with me. This will explain everything much more than words can."

What is he talking about?

I have to admit, my curiosity is peaked. I'm starting to think there's more to this than I initially thought. I mean, I did see - with my own two eyes - actual photographic proof of his family, so whatever excuse he has to explain it all away has to be pretty effing substantial.

Maybe I should see this for myself.

"Fine. I'll follow you, but I'm still wary, you got that?"

"Oh, super clear, Grace."

"Good, because nothing you can say will change my opinion of you."

I push away his hand. I'm not a child to be led down-stairs. I can do it on my own.

Duke chuckles quietly to himself. "I really like your bite, Grace."

I growl at him as he guides me back down the stairs. The priest from earlier is standing at the bottom of the stairs, clearly checking up on us. I don't blame him; I wouldn't trust us two with a bargepole. Duke flashes him a ruthless grin and the robed man scurries away. We exit the Cathedral and head around the corner towards the Tube station where my tour groups start from.

Duke doesn't say a word as we head down a street towards his parked car.

"Get in," he says, indicating to the passenger seat.

I hate being told what to do. Mom used to say I have an issue with authority.

But when that authority is a gorgeous hunk with a smile that can melt your heart, then I have little choice but to do what he says.

No matter what happens or what he says, he is still a cheating bastard.

I get into his car. Duke gets into the driver's seat.

And he starts the engine. I sit there and think of only one question.

Where the hell are we going?

21

EIGHT YEARS EARLIER

DUKE

Everything changed in my life when Damien Whitlock found out my secret.

It happened at boarding school when I was sixteen. School was an easy ride for me. I was like every other Heath-Harding boy when I arrived at the ancient place of learning. Athletic, sporty, and smart. A natural leader of men in the making. My family had sent boys to that same boarding school since its inception in medieval times, and I'm proud to say I upheld our proud tradition of excelling in everything our blood turns its hand to.

At that Hogwarts-like place, I was being groomed to be a pillar of society. Another Heath-Harding conquering the world. Another Lord.

And that's why there was so much pressure for me to

succeed at school. It wouldn't just be me that would be dishonored, it would be my family. My history. Every other pupil at school knew who I was. Everyone knew the expectations placed upon me.

Everyone, including Damien.

Unlike me, Damien was an orphan. He was not some famous family or a lineage that spread back hundreds of years. He didn't get in because of nepotism; Damien had gotten into the boarding school due to his brains. He'd gotten a full scholarship. Those things were rare at that elite institution, so Damien achieving one was special.

Basically, he was one smart cookie.

We were both in the same year, living together during term time in the same dorm. I didn't know where he went during the holidays; he never spoke of the family he didn't have nor the people he was living with now. He kept himself to himself, but still remained respected among the other boys, who were vicious when it came to the social pecking order.

The boarding school was ranked as one of the best in Britain and in the entire world. It had turned out an endless number of Prime Ministers and generals and royalty from all around the globe.

We were the next generation of leaders.

And we were vicious to each other.

Being a Heath-Harding meant that I came to the school already on top of the hierarchy, but from the minute I arrived, I made sure to cement that reputation. I was taller, bigger, stronger, faster, and smarter than anyone else, and I purposely proved that over and over again to any other schoolboy who dared challenge me.

It was my responsibility as an alpha to look after the lower boys in the school. I had to remain above the petty politics of those boys who fought over scraps to get up the ladder. I was on top of them all.

Which led to me looking after Matt.

If the social hierarchy in the school could be represented by a ladder with me on top, then Matt would be ten feet away from the bottom step. He was skinny and underdeveloped physically compared to the other boys. We didn't know what conditions he had exactly, but he found reading and writing much harder than an average boy his age. I mean, we were just teenage boys and not doctors. We couldn't diagnose what he had, but I made sure we all looked out for him. Well, the decent boys did.

Unfortunately, not everyone did.

Which leads me to the day Damien discovered my secret.

It was a sport class when the incident happened. Mr. Warwick was one of my least-liked teachers already, even before that day. He was one of the sports teachers at the boarding school, a big round man with a drooping mustache and a flair for launching into his infamous temper at the drop of a hat. I doubt he had much of a dating history. I doubt teaching sport to boys was his first choice at occupation in life as well.

All in all, Mr. Warwick was not a nice man.

And that sports class brought out the worst in him. He had decided, in that pea-sized brain of his, to pick on Matt for no reason. We were meant to be taking laps of the school's brand-new running track. Mr. Warwick was supposed to be timing.

But when our group of boys made our way back around to the starting line, we saw that he had pulled Matt to the side and was berating him for something. We figured exactly what it was when we got closer.

"You're refusing to run as fast as the other boys?" Mr. Warwick was yelling at Matt, his mustache bouncing around his face. "That's such a girly thing. Are you a girl, Matt? Are you refusing to be a man?"

Us group of boys continued our lap. Looking back now, I'm full of regret that I didn't stop and intervene. But I didn't. I just continued with the other boys, but that lap made me think. And it made me angry. Through the rest of the run around the track, I kept an eye out over the field at the teacher and student, watching intently. I couldn't hear what was being said, but I saw Mr. Warwick's face light up as red as a tomato. A peculiar trademark of his. Something was going on. He gave Matt a sports bag. I couldn't tell what was in it.

And then I watched Matt walk away from the teacher, towards the changing rooms. Maybe it wasn't as serious as I thought. Maybe it was just Mr. Warwick losing his temper for a few minutes like he always did, and then he had let Matt go.

We rounded the corner and passed the starting line again. Mr. Warwick was not looking at us as we jogged by him.

He was staring at the changing rooms.

A moment later, I realized what the teacher was waiting for.

Matt had reappeared from the changing rooms.

This time wearing something very different from the school's sports uniform.

A pink tutu.

"Fuck," I muttered under my breath. The other boys in the running group turned and saw what was going on. Some of them laughed. Not for long, though. I barked at them. They listened to me and fell back into line.

Matt strolled, nervous and embarrassed, out across the track towards Mr. Warwick. Tears were running down his face.

The boy was crying.

My hands balled into fists as I overheard some of the words spoken by the teacher.

Such a girl.

Dress you up like one.

See? This is who you are. Nice and pink.

You like wearing pink? I thought you might.

Pink is feminine, like you.

You're so weak, you know that?

Weak.

Girly. Girly.

Girl.

He'd made Matt dress up like this. For no real reason at all. He was making the boy cry for his own sick amusement, knowing full-well Matt's unique personality.

As I ran with the group of boys, I knew I had to do something about this. It made me angry in the pit of my stomach.

I couldn't confront Mr. Warwick straight away. Despite my strength, he was still a teacher. What I needed to do would have to be a whole lot more subtle. Send a clear message to the teacher that what he'd done was wrong.

Matt joined us then, running along completely out-of-breath in the stupid pink tutu.

He just kept repeating to us how sorry he was.

"Don't worry, Matt," I told him as we jogged around a bend. "You're doing fine. We are all here for you. Ignore Mr. Warwick."

"He told me I'm a girl, and he told me I had to dress up as one and that I deserve to be laughed at."

"No one here is laughing at you," I replied, shooting warning glances at the other boys. "No one. We have your back, Matt."

He wasn't really listening; he was too busy sobbing.

"I'm so sorry."

"You're doing fine, Matt. Stay with us. You're doing fine."

The whole thing was not fair, and I was determined - no matter *fucking* what - that Mr. Warwick was going to get what he deserved.

* * *

Mr. Warwick had a sports car that was his pride and joy. It was black. Jet black. Boy, did he fucking *love* that thing, showing it off whenever he could. Spending his free days washing it by hand very publicly in the middle of the teachers' parking lot.

The car seemed like the only thing in the world he cared about, except maybe his mustache.

I spent the rest of the day after Mr. Warwick had so carelessly humiliated Matt mulling over in my mind what I could do to avenge the schoolboy's embarrassment. How I could punish Mr. Warwick for the shitty thing he had done. What I could do to really make him see what a cunt he'd been to the weakest boy in the school.

And every plan always ended up coming back to that car of his.

If I wanted to hit him where it hurt, then that fucking monstrosity would be my best bet.

And so, the day ended, and we schoolboys were sent into our dorms on campus. Boarding school is a weird fucking place. No girls were even allowed within *sight* of our dorms, and that left a lot of teenage boys very horny. I didn't really care. Even at that age, I knew how to get pussy. It wasn't hard for a guy like me, but I digress.

Mr. Warwick's sports car. That was what I was saying.

Under the cover of night, when most of the boys were fast asleep around me, I snuck out of the dorms. It seemed like the only one still up was Matt, but he was too busy crying about the experience of the day to take notice of my shadow creeping out of the medieval-era building.

Poor lad.

I crossed the school, heading straight for the teachers' parking lot. Heading straight for Mr. Warwick's pride and joy.

I knew what I was there to do.

I'd brought along my backpack. Inside were two spray cans I'd bartered off another boy in my year for a box of cigarettes. I didn't smoke, but I always kept a few packets to haggle with in times of crisis.

The job on Mr. Warwick's car didn't take me too long. A few minutes later and the whole car had been vandalized. I'd sprayed in deep thick lines of pink over the black, cutting through it all with one giant word all in red.

WEAK.

Because that was who Mr. Warwick was for picking on Matt. A weak fucking man. And now it was there, on his car, for the whole world to see.

Matt wasn't weak. Mr. Warwick was.

Job done, I stood back and admired my handiwork in the darkness.

And then I spotted movement from inside the school grounds. Someone had been watching me. I squinted through the shadows to spot a figure running away, but it was too late for them. I knew who they were.

Damien.

He and I hadn't really spoken to each other. There had been a mutual respect between the two of us ever since he'd arrived on that full scholarship. I respected his intelligence and hard work, and he respected my natural leadership and alpha status within the school. We're barely even said two words to each other beyond a friendly nod when we passed in the school hallways.

But now everything had changed. He'd seen me damage a teacher's property. Worse than that. He'd *witnessed* me *vandalizing* Mr. Warwick's prized car.

That crime was an expellable offense. Which meant one thing.

I had to chase after him.

And so I did.

* * *

I FOUND DAMIEN PRETTY EASILY. He'd snuck back into the dorms, back into his room. He was there as I entered, sitting on his bed fully dressed like he was expecting me.

There was no panic. No rush. Both of us knew the situation. We knew how to deal with each other as gentlemen. There was no need to come to blows. Yet.

I closed his bedroom door behind me and stood to my full height.

"You saw it all?" I asked Damien quietly.

"Yes."

The moonlight streaming in from outside revealed his handsome features. He was going to become a very good-looking man.

"You know what would happen if that came back to me?"

Damien didn't look frightened of me. He kept his eye contact and nodded again.

"I know who you are. I know your family. I know what the school will do to you and what that means for you within your family."

"Right," I replied. "So, you do know."

"I do."

"Good. Then you know I will get expelled?"

"Yes."

"I can't let that happen to me," I replied. "What are you going to do about it?"

He could demand nearly anything he wanted from me, and I would oblige him without question. The last thing I needed in my life was to be expelled from this place. My reputation would be in irreparable tatters. I would be cast out of the family by my father. You might think that's unreasonable or unrealistic, but you probably haven't grown up in a noble family with a history stretching back to William the Conqueror. It would happen to me.

And Damien knew it.

He took a long time to answer. I saw him thinking about it over in his head. If I had any doubts about his intelligence, then I didn't after that pause.

He must've known he had me by the balls. He must've known he could crush me with a single word. At that moment, he had my entire life in his hands.

My heart beat faster and faster every second he was silent.

"What Mr. Warwick did to Matt was wrong. Very wrong," he replied eventually.

"Are you going to tell?" I asked him.

Damien didn't reply. He just held his stare into my eyes for a moment before lying back on his bed.

"Close the door on the way out," he replied.

And then he shut his eyes, and I knew then he wasn't going to utter another word.

And I spent the night sleepless, not knowing what my fate was going to be. I had tried to avenge a boy under my care, but now I was potentially going to get expelled.

Still, I was ready to accept whatever consequences. I knew I had done the right thing. Someone needed to show Mr. Warwick a lesson.

* * *

THE NEXT MORNING, we were all awoken to the angry screaming of Mr. Warwick as he saw his car in the sunlight. I was already lying in bed - having not slept - waiting for the teacher's reaction.

And it didn't disappoint.

Soon, everyone in the school had gathered outside to see what the hell was going on. Everyone saw the spray paint. The message I had left for Mr. Warwick.

Everyone knew what it meant.

And then there were calls over the loudspeaker for an emergency morning assembly. Just as I expected.

We all gathered in the school's chapel for what was to be a chaotic morning assembly. Mr. Warwick ran it, running around and yelling at the gathered boys. He practically had to be restrained by the other teachers as he demanded the culprit to come forward or he will summon the police. Tell all our parents. He made countless threats. My vandalism had clearly really gotten to him, and for that I was proud.

It made me even more proud to see that Matt was standing at the back of the chapel, smiling. I'd made him feel strong again.

That's why I did what I did.

I tried to spot Damien in the crowd, to try to see how he may react to all of this. To the threats. But he was nowhere to be seen.

Maybe he was already talking to the headmaster. Maybe I was already a goner.

The assembly only ended when the head English teacher managed to wrangle an out-of-control Mr. Warwick and announce to the gathered boys that whoever was responsible for the crime would have one hour to report themselves to the headmaster or police will have to participate.

I knew what the honorable thing was to do right then. I may have gotten expelled for it, but I was raised by Camilla to tell the truth. To face the world as a man with your shoulders back and no lie upon my lips. To defend the weak and uphold my dignity. I wasn't going to forego that now.

The assembly was broken up, and I made my solemn way across the school towards the headmaster's office.

But there was already someone there. Someone leaving the office as I climbed the stairs to reach it.

Damien.

"What have you done?" I asked him, confused. "I am going to own up."

He looked at me then, his face stern and uncompromising. "It's too late. If you speak out now, then both of us will get the punishment. Don't waste your opportunity."

"What? What have you done, Damien?"

"What do you think I've done?"

"I did that to the car. I deserve to face the punishment. You can't take it for me."

"Duke, face the obvious. It's better for me to get expelled and not the next Lord Heath-Harding. It's too late now to change things. Go back to your classroom."

And then he passed me. I watched him leave in shock.

And that was when everything changed in my life. When Damien knew what I had done and yet took the fall for it.

He knew my secret, and yet still saved my life.

No matter what, I owed him a debt. Something that I'm still paying off.

And that explains everything Grace wants to know.

22

PRESENT DAY

GRACE

WHAT THE HELL is it that Duke just told me? What the hell was that story?

Sure, it was nice to hear of something that's happened in his past, but what does it all *mean*?

And why does he feel the need to tell me about it at all? At this time?

All these questions roll about in my head as I sit beside him in the car as we zoom out of London. Green fields pass by the window as I grow even more irritated by what is going on.

Where is he taking me and why is he babbling on about his schooldays?

I sit there with my arms crossed as he talks. It's an interesting tale, for sure, but why does this man insist on being so goddamn *mysterious*?

Why can't he just give me a straight answer?

"You said you were going to explain yourself," I mutter to Duke as he stoically steers the car down winding country lanes. "None of what you just said has explained either sleeping with me under nefarious pretenses or the fact you've got a family you've kept hidden."

"It does explain everything," he replies coolly. "If you let me continue."

"I don't know why I'm even letting you."

"You'll see."

"Where are you even taking me?"

"You'll see."

Yeah, like I said. *Mysterious.*

Why did I agree to get into this car? Is he just going to dump me off in some field to make my way back to the city? Is this all some sick practical joke?

I wouldn't put that past Duke.

"*I'll see?*"

"Damien immediately joined the military after he was expelled," Duke continues, ignoring my frustration. "It was the only option left to an orphan with no money and no family to turn to. It was a good thing for him. He was good at the army life, rising through the ranks quickly. He was smart and resourceful. A natural leader. Despite our distance apart, Damien and I kept in touch over the years. I never forgot the debt I owed him, and I wanted to make sure he knew that, so I reached out to him. We became best friends through our correspondence with each other over the years. I was Best Man at his wedding to his beautiful wife. I was godfather to his first child."

Duke goes silent then for a moment. I don't dare interrupt him. He looks like he's on the verge of tears, which shakes me. I never thought I might see this man so hurt by something.

"I was also the lead pallbearer of the coffin at his funeral," Duke says quietly. He's trying to hold back emotion, but his voice betrays him with a light crackle. "You see, Damien died on a military tour overseas, leaving his wife and young children behind. His new family. They were the people you saw in those photos. The family you thought was mine."

Oh.

And then everything dawns on me.

And I realize what an idiot I've been.

I sit in complete shock, not moving at all.

Duke doesn't say another word until he slows down the car in front of a secluded house.

"We're here. Let me show you what this all means."

"Duke..."

I start, but he doesn't let me continue. He sternly raises a hand.

"No one else knows about this, not even my brother. I would like it to be kept secret, you understand?"

I nod, unable to find the right words to say to him.

Duke turns off the ignition and I follow him to the front door of the house. It sits on its own out in the country. We're surrounded by rolling green hills and hedges. A perfect English slice of heaven.

Duke knocks on the door. A woman our age answers. She smiles warmly at Duke and gives him a big, hearty hug.

She's the woman from the photos. The woman I thought was Duke's bride.

"Grace, this is Audrey Whitlock," Duke says, introducing us. "Damien's wife."

* * *

"Here's your tea," Audrey says as she hands me a steaming mug. I take it from her with a smile.

"Thank you."

"It's nice that you two came to visit," she says. "It's *always* nice when Duke comes to see us. He's such fun for the kids. They absolutely adore him. I like watching them play together. He brings a much-needed ray of sunshine into their lives whenever he's here."

She nods to the kitchen window. Duke's currently outside with Audrey's two children, playing with them. He's in the middle of lifting them up in the air one-by-one, spinning them about before bringing them back down to earth. The air is full of the sound of their giggles and Duke's booming laughter.

It's a heartwarming sight to see, and something I would never in a million years picture Duke doing.

There's been a whole other side to the man I've had to come to terms with in the last hour. He's completely changed in front of me, from a heartless cheating bastard to this honorable provider for a family that isn't even his.

When Damien died, he took them under his wing, trying his best to pay off the debt he feels like he owes the boy who saved him from being expelled.

"I didn't know Duke was such a kid-friendly person," I say. Audrey laughs.

"You would never expect it from such a tall, silent man, I guess."

"No. Not him. Certainly not."

"But he's been such a good surrogate father to Jack and Anna."

I nod. "I can see that."

Looking at the tall man play and giggle with the kids makes me realize that I really do see it.

He's definitely not the man I thought he was.

Audrey leans in close like she's about to tell me a secret.

"He would hate me telling you this, but he pays for their education, you know."

"Really? Wow."

"They're going to go to the same school as Damien and Duke went to. He says he's going to make sure of that. He wants to give them the best education in the country. Duke might present a hard exterior, but he really loves them. I think he loves them more than anything else in the world."

Audrey takes a drink from her tea and stares longingly out the window at Duke and the kids. I can see what Duke's kindness means to her. The whole world.

There's this entire side of the man that's hidden from everyone else – even his brother - and he's decided to show *me* it. What does that mean? What do I mean to him?

"Was this place yours and Damien's?" I ask, looking around at the lovely country home. "It's so pretty."

Audrey shakes her head. "No. Definitely not. This place is a considerable upgrade to the place we shared. Duke set up this place for us when Damien passed. I resisted as much as I can, but you really can't say no to him, can't you?"

I roll my eyes. "Oh, I definitely know that."

"Despite me resisting him at every stage of getting this place, Duke always kept saying that Damien would do the same for him if the positions were reversed, and that's true. He never takes a no from me. Ever. We want for nothing here."

"He's pretty bone-headed," I say. "If there's one thing I've learned about Duke in the last few days, it's that he's pretty persistent."

"That's for sure."

"Are those pictures of Damien?" I ask, pointing at a row of photographs above the kitchen sink. Audrey turns to them and smiles weakly.

There are photos of him in his military uniform. One of him with Audrey and the kids. One of him and Duke raising beers in a pub.

"Yes. Oh, you would've loved Damien, Grace. He was like Duke, strong but gentle. Headstrong but loving. The life of the party when he got going."

"He sounds like a perfect gentleman."

"He was. We never got to spend a lifetime together, but the few years we did have were a gift and a blessing," Audrey says. A single tear runs down her cheek. "I, for one, know how lucky it is to find a good man. Duke is a good man. You're a very lucky girlfriend."

I blush. "Thank you," I manage to say.

It's a little lie, but I don't want to ruin the mood by saying to her that I'm not Duke's girlfriend. I don't want to tell her that – just this morning – I actually hated his guts.

I quickly sip my tea and look back out the window at Duke and kids playing in the field.

I was so wrong about him. So unbelievably wrong. And I was blinded by my rage.

With him and the kids, it's like I'm seeing him for the first time again.

Who is this man?

23

GRACE

DUKE DOESN'T TELL Audrey about either the murder or the threats against his family. Instead, we spend the time at her house chatting about other things. Lighter topics.

"How are Anna and Jack doing at school?" he asks her as we sit in the living room and drink tea together. The kids continue playing outside.

Audrey shows him the kids' latest report cards, and Duke scans through them with a curious intensity.

I just sit there and think about how caring this man is for children that aren't even his. He really feels like he owes Damien a lifetime debt. He's doing the honorable thing.

He's a good man, and I was so damn wrong about him.

"These are good," Duke says. "You've done an amazing job with them. They're top of their classes."

"They try hard at school," Audrey replies. "They're really happy there."

Duke nods. "Thanks to you."

"No, thanks to *you*."

Audrey serves us a constant stream of tea and delicious cake. Soon it's time to leave. My bladder is thankful.

Audrey gathers the kids at the doorway to say goodbye. They sprint through the house.

"Nice to meet you two," I say to Jack and Anna. They both smile cheekily at me, looking just like their father in the photos I've seen. I shake their little hands. They're so mature for their ages. "Behave yourselves."

"Bye, Miss Madden."

Then it's Duke's time to say goodbye. He lifts them both in the air with his strong arms and chucks them around, much to their giggling delight. He's so annoyingly good with kids. They're attracted to his boisterous energy, a side of him I doubt many people in the cutthroat business world have witnessed.

We head out the front door, and Duke pulls Audrey aside to speak to her quietly. As I pass, I overhear what he's asking her.

"You all okay? Do you need anything?"

"I'm okay, Duke. Totally fine."

"You sure? You know you can ask me for anything, right?"

"I know. Thank you, Duke."

"Alright."

I smile to myself and walk over to the car. Audrey follows me, giving me a big hug.

"Take care of him," she whispers in my ear.

"Oh, I will. Don't you worry about that."

I wink at Duke. He doesn't know what we're saying to each other, and he looks at us, confused. I like holding a secret from him.

He and Audrey hug, and then we get into his car.

We wave to the kids gathered at Audrey's side and drive out of there, back towards London.

In the quiet of the car, I place my hand on Duke's knee and turn to him.

"Duke. First, I need to say I'm sorry about..."

He cuts me off.

"It's fine, Grace."

"But about me accusing you of..."

"It is totally fine, Grace. I can see why you would assume the worst of me. It's a complete miscommunication. It was not your fault."

"But four years of thinking you were *that*. I really didn't know the real reason. I'm just so sorry to have thought so many bad things about you."

Duke's blue eyes gleam at me. "Don't you apologize for anything, Grace. You have nothing to apologize for. You thought I was someone I'm not, and it's understandable."

"But *four years*?" I shake my head, laughing at my own stupidity. "You should've told me something."

Duke winks at me. "I tried to find you, but you blocked me on all social media, remember?"

"Oh. Right. Yeah."

He chuckles and changes gear. "But then we've found each other, so it all worked out in the end, right?"

I smile at him. "Yeah, it did."

"You know, if Damien didn't stand up for me - if he didn't take the fall for something I'd done - then I would not be the man I am today, I'm sure of it," Duke says quietly. "I would not be in the job I'm in, making the kind of money I make. I feel like I owe everything to Damien. And now that he's gone, I owe it to him to look after his family."

"You're a good man, Duke."

He scoffs at that. "I was a coward a few years ago and let that boy take the consequences I should've faced. Helping Damien's family is the very least I can do."

"Well, you look after them well."

"I hope so," Duke replies.

"You do. You really do."

Duke takes in a deep breath. "You have to promise me something though, Grace."

"What?"

His voice goes quiet. "I need you to be silent about this. I need you not to say a word about Damien or his family to anyone else, especially to my brother. I don't like what I'd done back at boarding school. I hate how he'd taken the fall for me. The tabloids would have a field day if they found out, and we both know they wouldn't understand. They'll think I've got a hidden family or something. They'll think the kids are mine. It'll be a scandal I can't afford to have."

"I understand," I reply. "I swear I'll keep it between us. But even your brother?"

Duke slowly nods. "I don't want anyone knowing. Not even King."

"Why don't you just tell him? I'm sure he'll understand."

"I'm just... *ashamed* of what Damien had to do for me. It wasn't exactly the most honorable thing to do."

"I'm really sure King would get it."

Duke turns back to me, his face cold. "I don't want him to know."

"Okay," I reply. "If that's what you wish, then I won't utter a single word about it. To anybody."

We drive along in silence for a while. I mull over what Duke's saying to me.

I will keep my word, though. I will keep Audrey and the kids safe from the outside world.

"How about you tell me a secret," Duke suggests as London comes into view on the horizon.

"What?"

"Well, now that you know a secret about me, how about

I know something about you? So that we're even. It'll help me feel better."

I chuckle and shake my head. "I don't have any secrets, Duke. I'm an open book."

"Oh, I'm sure you have something."

"Nope."

"Anything?"

I shuffle in the car seat and smile weakly. "Well, there is something. I'm not sure how much of a secret it really is, but it's something I won't share with anyone unless they were special to me."

"Wait, so you're saying I'm special?"

"Shut up," I say, pinching his shoulder.

"Go on, then. Tell me this half-secret of yours, Miss Madden."

"I miss my mom."

Duke doesn't reply. He just reaches over and runs his hand through my hair.

"I miss her so freaking much," I continue. "She was my best friend. My only friend. I guess my secret would be that I haven't had a proper friend like my mom until Scarlett came into my life. Sure, I know a lot of people. But no one has been as close to me as my mother until I met Scarlett."

"Grace, I'm sorry."

"No. Don't be," I reply. To my surprise, tears start welling up. Duke wipes them away on the back of his finger. "Mom told me a story once. How she went backpacking around Europe when she was my age now. She went to Italy. To Rome. She managed to get into the Sistine Chapel and looked up at the ceiling that Michelangelo painted. She told me that, at that moment, her whole life seemed to stop. She saw the beauty in everything. She said that the Sistine Chapel was her favorite place in the entire world. I would love to visit it someday."

"I'm sure you will," Duke says.

"It's what I'm saving up for as I work for the tour company. A trip to Rome."

Duke laughs. "Don't you mean *my* tour company now?"

I roll my eyes.

This fucking man.

He can make me go from warming my heart seeing him with Damien's kids one minute to making me so damn annoyed with him the next.

And this is the moment I know I'm falling for him.

24

GRACE

"Wait, what are you saying?" Scarlett asks me as we walk through Notting Hill Market, browsing through the display of each stall as we pass. "You're saying that Duke is *not* a major dick?"

"Exactly," I reply, stopping at one market stall, glancing over the mirrors on sale. Multiple reflections of Scarlett and I glare back at me. I reckon some of these would look great in our flat hallway. "He's not what I thought he was."

"What do you mean?"

"I can't really tell you why, but I was wrong about Duke. So very wrong."

"You can't tell me why?"

"Nope."

"Oh, so sneaky of you, Grace."

"You know me. I like being mysterious. I'm pretty cool."

"So, you were wrong about him. What are you going to do now? How do you feel about him?"

Those two questions make me laugh loudly, scaring the

stall seller sitting next to me. I apologize to them and turn to Scarlett.

"Those are the two things that I can't get out of my head. How do I feel about him and what the hell I'm going to do next."

"Well, do you *like* him?" my best friend asks me.

I pause.

I immediately want to tell her that *yes*. I do like him. My body wants him all the fucking time. I can't get the man's face out of my head. I just can't stop thinking about Duke Heath-Harding. I look into his sharp blue eyes and all I see is him and I together.

But at the same time, I don't want to admit that, not even to my best friend. I don't want to give in too quickly to a man I thought I hated for four years.

"I've had to absorb a lot of new information about Duke in the last day," I tell her. "A freaking lot. It's like I'm suffering from whiplash. I don't know where my head is at."

We continue past the mirror stall and up the road to a crossing. We stop at the pedestrian red light and wait for the traffic to pass.

"Come on, Grace," Scarlett tells me sternly. "I never took you as someone to not be direct or make up your mind. You're a go-getter. You either like him or you don't. It's that simple."

"Scarlett..."

She grabs my hand.

"Grace. You like him or you don't. What is it?"

I open my mouth, about to utter my answer, when a car screeches to a stop in front of us. Both Scarlett and I freeze in shock.

What the fuck...

The window winds down.

"Duke?" I ask, dumbfounded.

The man is sitting behind the wheel, staring at us both with those irresistible eyes of his.

"Duke?" Scarlett repeats.

"Hello, girls."

Oh, he certainly *loves* how he's dramatically come to a stop in front of us. He probably thinks of himself as suave as James Bond with that little stunt of his.

And the infuriating thing is that he wouldn't be wrong.

"What are you doing here?" I ask him. "How did you even know we would be here? How did you find us?"

He shrugs. "I'm just an amazing detective, I guess."

"Bullshit."

"Oh, but I am. I'm better than your favorite Sherlock Holmes, Grace. Either that or maybe the fact King knew where you two would be and he told me."

"Great," Scarlett says, rolling her eyes. "That boy is gonna pay for that when I see him next."

"You're *impossible*, Duke," I tell him. "You know that, right?"

"That's enough of a day out for the both of you. I'm going to steal you." He nods to the passenger seat next to him. "Shut up and get in, Grace."

25

DUKE

THE FIRST THING Grace asks when she gets into my car makes me laugh.

"You're not kidnapping me, are you?"

"No."

"Well, what about Scarlett?" she continues, waving towards her friend waiting on the pavement outside the car.

Scarlett bends down to window height before I can answer. "I'm fine," she tells Grace.

"No, you're not. I'm not leaving you alone. Get in."

"She's fine," I say to Grace.

"Stop being so rude," she barks back at me. "I'm not leaving her on her own."

Scarlett laughs. "I'm truly fine, Grace. I'll get a taxi back to King's."

Grace's eyes narrow. "You sure?"

"You two have a good time. Take good care of her, Duke."

I nod at Scarlett and then put my foot down on the pedal, joining the traffic heading out of Notting Hill.

I take in Grace sitting next to me. I want her. All of her. Right now, I just want to kiss her full lips and feel her tits. It's so intoxicating sitting next to someone you know you can't have.

She's seen my most intimate secret. Damien's family. I let her into something I've never shown anyone else. I've been more vulnerable in front of her than I've been with my own family.

Grace, it is safe to say, is not like any other girl.

And we still haven't spoken about what we truly want for each other.

Well, I want her.

But does she want me?

That question has been burning in my head ever since I dropped her home after meeting Audrey and the kids.

And now I'm going to get my answer. I've not been able to think of anything else for the last day. I need to know what she's thinking.

"Where are you taking me?" Grace asks.

"You'll see."

"You really like saying that, don't you, Duke? You think you're so cool and sexy when you're being so secretive."

"Are you saying I'm not sexy and cool?"

Grace falls silent and I smile to myself.

"I got you this," I say, reaching over to the passenger seat behind me.

"What is it?"

I hand Grace a rose. She stares at me, gripping it between her fingers.

"It's like you; beautiful but also full of thorns."

"Thank you," she replies. "No one has ever got me a flower before."

I smirk. "Well, now I'm your first."

"Shut up, Duke."

"And *there's* that thorny side of you," I reply. "Right on time."

"Just focus on the road and try not to kill us both," she retorts.

I chuckle and change gear.

I wouldn't change that thorny side of her for the world.

* * *

IT DOESN'T TAKE LONG to get to where we're going.

Harrods.

The giant luxury department store in one of the richest parts of the capital. Famous for its expensive products and history. This building is the king of department stores, and I'm taking Grace there.

She can't hide her gasp of astonishment as my car pulls up alongside the building.

"We're going there?" she asks.

"Yep. You ever been?"

"I've always been too scared to step inside."

"Why?"

"Oh, I've always felt not rich or posh enough to go through those doors," Grace says.

"Screw that. You're coming in with me. You should have no problem at all not thinking you're important enough. Those doormen will practically *bow* with you on my arm."

"Cocky boy," Grace replies.

I open her door and help her out. We then march through the front doors of Harrods with me holding her hand. The doormen don't even question Grace. To them, we're a high-flying couple coming in to shop and we should be treated with that respect.

"Mr. Heath-Harding."

A man dressed in a suit appears by our side. I recognize him. He's there to greet VIPs who visit the department store. Grace just stares up at him, blinking. She's really never been treated like this before.

"Hello."

"How may I be of assistance today, sir and madam?"

I wave him away. "I'm just browsing here with my girl," I reply. I feel Grace's eyes fall on me as I call her mine. "We have no need for assistance."

"Very well, sir."

Grace waits for the suited man to walk away before she raises an eyebrow at me.

"*My girl*?"

"After today, you will be."

"You think?"

"I *know* it."

"Oh, you're not just a cocky boy, Duke. You're *arrogant*."

I grin at her, and she scoffs sarcastically.

She doesn't realize how right I am. She *is* going to be my girl by the end of today. I've waited four years for this moment and I'm not going to let it go.

I guide Grace up to the next floor. Womenswear. Here are some of the best dresses from the top designers in the world. Dresses so expensive that I can understand why some people like Grace would freak out over even entering this shop.

She just sighs when she sees the display; it's too much for her to take in.

"Can we have a look around?" she asks me.

"That's why we're here, Grace. Look around to your heart's delight."

We spend the next hour browsing through every dress on offer. I love every minute of it. Seeing Grace's face light up makes everything worthwhile. She tries on a few dresses and marvels at how nice everything is. I just stand back and watch.

"This is just a taste of what it'll be like to be my girl," I whisper to her after she tries on another elegant dress that suits her perfectly. Grace's mouth just hangs open, too engrossed in the dresses to deliver a snarky comment back at me.

My intentions are fully out in the open now. It's up to her to give her heart to me.

Grace pulls out a dress. It's a gown with a side split. Silver and embellished. I call over the assistant.

"You want to try it on?" I ask Grace.

She shrugs. "Won't hurt."

She's trying to downplay her excitement, but she's failing.

Grace disappears to the changing room and returns moments later with the dress on.

I freeze.

"You look like a princess," I say to her, my breath knocked out of my body by the sight of her.

She really does. The gown hugs her body's curves perfectly. She looks elegant. A million dollars.

A girl worthy enough to be a Heath-Harding.

"Thank you." Grace blushes.

"You can pick anything you want in here," I say to her. "Anything, and I'll give it to you. I'm made of money."

Grace frowns at me and steps closer.

"One thing to get straight, Duke, is that I'm not your trophy wife, nor will I ever be. You can't impress me with your money, you got that? I don't give a shit about your money at all. The only thing I care about is what is in here."

She points a finger at my chest.

At my heart.

Boy, she's a tough nut to crack.

"What do you want, then?" I ask her.

Grace smiles, knowing she has the upper hand.

"That's the million pound question you'll just have to figure out for yourself, isn't it? What I want," she continues. "But you can make a start by being true to your word and getting me this gown."

Damn.

She's got me there.

This girl knows how to play me like a fucking fiddle.

26

GRACE

THE THEATER IS abuzz with the sound of an audience again. Weeks after it was forced to close due to the murder of Ben Helper, the Prestige Theater is back. With Kingsley's play back on.

"This is crazy, though," I whisper to Scarlett as we make our way inside the auditorium. "We still haven't discovered who the murderer is yet. Whoever killed Ben is still at large and King is back doing his show."

"King tells me they have strict security operating here," she replies. We search for our seats up the aisle. "He's not worried. He tells me he doesn't want to be cowed by some madman who's full of empty threats. No hiding from the world. He wants to continue his career."

"I can't blame him," I say. "But it's pretty risky."

"He's a Heath-Harding. Those boys do whatever they want to."

I roll my eyes. "Oh, how I've come to know *that* in the last few days."

We stumble across our seats. They're right in the front of the auditorium, so very close to the stage. Of course they are. Only the best for the girlfriend of the star.

I've come not because of Duke, but to support Scarlett. Despite her assurances, I'm still completely confused why they're putting the play back on when the murderer still walks amongst us.

Scarlett no longer works here. She doesn't want to be working at the same place her boyfriend performs at every night. Fair enough, I think.

So now we're here for the re-opening of Kingsley's play, and the theater is full. So many celebrities are here, and Scarlett and I have been put ahead of them in the best seats in the house.

Scarlett is clearly the most important thing in King's life.

We sit, nursing the wines we bought at the bar. Soon enough, the curtain rises. The theater darkens. The play begins to rapturous applause.

"That's Penelope Jellis," Scarlett whispers to me as a beautiful blonde woman strolls on stage. I'm mesmerized by her. God, she's out of this world. She reminds me of some Hollywood starlet in the thirties.

I don't need Scarlett to remind me who the woman is. She's King's co-star in the play. An actress who became insanely jealous of Scarlett's relationship with King. She thought she deserved him instead of my best friend.

Ha.

How very wrong she was.

Scarlett and King deserve each other. I don't just know it; I've witnessed it with my own eyes. They've stayed at our flat a few times. I've spied them watching films together and cuddling like two kittens.

I've seen how Kingsley treats Scarlett as a princess, which is exactly what she is.

Their love for each other is boundless. They're a perfect couple.

So. Yeah. Penelope has every right to be jealous of their relationship. Hell, I practically am.

The play continues. King appears. Just like Scarlett has told me a million times, he is an amazing actor. So damn charismatic and cool. He's a natural on stage. I bet there are big things for his career in the future. The next Brad Pitt? For sure.

During the performance, I feel someone watching me from behind. I turn in my seat to look.

Duke is directly two rows behind me. His attention is not on the stage, but on me.

I glance away, awkward. I turn back to the stage. He knows how to get under my skin. I can't stop thinking about him.

I sit completely still for the rest of the play, always feeling Duke's deep blue eyes on me.

Don't get turned on, Grace. Not here. Not now. Even if there's the most gorgeous man on the planet sitting behind you undoubtedly thinking naughty things about you.

The performance ends to a standing ovation. Everyone has risen out of their seats and is clapping enthusiastically, and for good reason. It's a triumph. Both Scarlett and I whistle at King as he takes his bows alongside Penelope. He spots us in the audience and winks. Scarlett cheers like the uber proud girlfriend she is.

The applause continues for what seems like an eternity until King eventually raises his hands, hushing the audience so that he can speak.

"Thank you all for coming to this re-opening," he says from the middle of the stage. "As you all probably know, there's been a tragic incident here. You've probably even heard about the threat against my life, but I want to tell you all that I will not be threatened by anyone. They'll have to come and get me, and I'm prepared to put up a fight."

The audience launches into applause again. King smiles and hushes us.

"But now there's something more important for me to deal with," he says, his voice lowering. "Something much, *much* more important. Where is Scarlett Hart?"

Next to me, my best friend freezes. I grab her hand and she squeezes. She's as shocked as I am.

I think we both know what's happening, but she's petrified to the spot.

I guess she needs her best friend to give her a little push.

I raise her hand up in the air and squeal out loud.

"She's here."

King chuckles and beckons her over.

"Come up here, Scarlett."

My best friend turns and looks me in the eye.

"*Grace...*"

She murmurs my name softly. Her voice is full of excitement and trepidation. I just smile and her and nod.

"Go."

She passes through the row and King offers her a helping hand onto the stage. She stands there, self-consciously, in the middle of the stage as everyone stares. Everyone is silent, watching her and King and what is about to unfold.

"Scarlett Hart," King says. "You've been the best thing to have ever happen in my life. Meeting you all those years ago and then getting another chance all these years later has been a blessing beyond my wildest dreams. You are a miracle. You deserve the world."

And then, in front of Scarlett and the entire audience, he gets down on one knee. He produces a ring from a pocket in his costume.

Tears are streaming down Scarlett's face, which makes me start to cry.

People may say magical moments only belong in fiction, but this is real life. And it's happening right in front of me.

"Scarlett Hart," King begins. We all definitely know where this is going now. "Will you marry me?"

27

GRACE

Scarlett says yes.

I mean, of course she does. Who wouldn't reject a wedding proposal from Kingsley Heath-Harding, especially when it is as romantically swoony as doing it in a hundred-year-old theater?

The whole room erupts into applause when she nods at Kingsley, tears streaming down her face. Tears are streaming down mine as well. I don't think there's a dry eye in the entire theater.

And then it's just chaos. Kingsley bows again to the audience before leaving the stage with Scarlett. The curtain comes down. Everyone starts gossiping and talking amongst themselves as they head out the exits in one mass.

I mean, Kingsley does know how to put on a show, doesn't he? A natural entertainer.

Instead of following everyone else out, I head to a side door that I know leads backstage. I squeeze my way out of the crowd and into the quiet of the many narrow corridors that lead behind the theater.

I'm looking for my best friend. The only time I've been back here was when I investigated the empty theater in the dark and surprised Scarlett. At least this time there's light.

I rush along until I find Kingsley's dressing room. It's pretty obvious it's his. The name is printed across the door.

I knock and hear Scarlett's voice cry out to come in.

It's just her alone in there. She's standing, clearly in such surprise that she doesn't know what to do with herself or her body.

"Grace?"

She calls out my name when she sees me, happiness spreading across her face. I sprint over and envelop her in a massive bear hug. We hold each other tight.

"That was insane," I whisper into her ear.

"I can't believe it, Grace. I really can't believe it. He asked me to marry him. I'm getting *married*."

"I am so incredibly happy for you, Scarlett."

"Thank you."

"You two make the cutest couple. I don't think I've ever met a better pairing."

"Grace, stop it. You're making me blush."

"But this means one thing, doesn't it?"

"What?"

I sigh. "This means you won't be my flatmate anymore, right?"

Scarlett laughs. "Grace, I think the wedding will be quite some time away. You're not getting rid of me just yet. We've still got plenty of time together."

"Yep, we do."

"We'll always have each other, no matter what."

"We do," I reply. "Gosh, I'm just so happy for you, Scarlett."

"It's my dreams come true."

"I know."

"People might think it's happened so fast, but I just *know* that it's right that King and I are together."

"Screw what other people think," I reply seriously. "You're following your heart, Scarlett. That's all that matters."

"Thanks, Grace. I'm glad you're here with me."

"I'm glad I'm here too."

There's another knock on the door, and then everyone in the entire freaking world seems to swarm into the dressing room.

They all congratulate my best friend. She looks so overwhelmed with everything. Her tears from the stage are still glistening on her cheeks as she tries to smile at all the guests. I keep holding her hand tight to remind her that I'm close. That she can rely on me.

Even bloody Penelope is here, smiling with all the fake humility in the world at Scarlett. I roll my eyes at the woman, making my distaste well known.

"Congratulations, Scarlett."

Congratulations, my ass, Penelope.

From the doorway, I see my best friend's old boss, and theater manager of the Prestige – Giles - speak up. I met him once before, at the press night for the play, just after Scarlett moved in with me.

God, that seems like a long time ago. Back when Scarlett and I were both pissed at each Heath-Harding brother.

I remember Scarlett telling me back then that Giles was so star-struck over the actors in the play. Well, I guess that, soon enough, Scarlett will probably be just as famous as Kingsley if she's gonna get married to him. She better get used to all this crazy attention.

Passing by Giles into the room like a giant, Duke

appears. He heads straight for Scarlett through the mob of people without a second glance, giving her a big hug in front of everyone.

"Welcome to the family," he says, winking at her. "It's rare to find a girl who can tame a Heath-Harding."

"Thank you, Duke."

"If you need anything, let me know. You're family now."

"Thanks."

And then King is here. Seeing the commotion and the effect it's having on poor Scarlett; he hushes everyone down.

"Thank you all for saying hello," he says as the room falls silent. "As you can imagine, there's a lot to plan and a lot for us to talk about. I'll get round to each of you in the next few days, but for now, I would love to have a few moments of peace with my bride-to-be, if that's okay?"

It's not a suggestion, but an order. And everyone knows that. They all stream out of the dressing room, leaving Duke, Kingsley, Scarlett, and me alone in the room.

I try to pull away to leave, to give them all some space, but Scarlett holds onto me.

"You're not going anywhere," she whispers to me.

"I'll leave you alone to be with your family," I reply.

"No. You're as much family as Duke is. Stay here."

I smile back at her. "Okay."

My heart warms up. I know we're going to be best friends for a very long time. *For life.*

"I love you," I tell her.

"I love you too, Grace," she replies. "Obviously, you're going to be Maid of Honor at the wedding."

"What? Me?"

"Of course. Who else would I choose?"

Tears are rolling down my cheeks. I may be acquainted with so many people in London. Nearly every bouncer in

Soho. People I've worked with. All the dates I've been on around the city. But I've never had as close a friend as Scarlett. For her to ask me to be her Maid of Honor is something I will never forget. It's a big bloody deal.

"Thank you, Scarlett."

She wipes the tears from my cheeks. "Don't thank me just yet, miss. I'm expecting a fun bachelorette party," she replies.

"You know me, Scarlett. You know my ways. We are going to have a very *dirty* night out. Trust me."

We turn back to the boys to tell them the good news, but they're already talking about something.

Something very serious.

"You should lie low," Duke is telling his brother.

"No, Duke. I'm not changing my life because of some loser."

"This guy's threats should not be taken lightly."

"I know."

"Then for Scarlett's sake. You got to protect her."

"I'm a big girl," she butts in. "I can fend for myself, boys."

"Of course you can," Duke replies. "But I'm just saying to keep low for a while, at least until we can catch this asshole."

"I agree," I say. "This guy is going to make a mistake if he keeps sending you threats. It's only a matter of time until we catch him. We have to play safe for now."

"Exactly right," Duke says.

"So, what's the plan?" King asks.

Duke stands tall, wrapping his arm around my shoulder and drawing me into his body.

"Grace and I are going to find this guy. Together."

28

GRACE

ONE OF LIFE's simple pleasures for me is drinking a nice mug of tea and watching true crime documentaries in my dressing gown.

And that's exactly what I'm doing now. Lazing around on my couch with the TV on and a large mug of steaming milky tea in between my hands. No makeup on. Not planning on seeing anyone at all today. My hair a crazy mess.

And it is absolute bliss.

The flat is empty. Scarlett is out today. She spent last night with King. Obviously. And today he's taking her for a spa day at a luxury London hotel. She's bloody lucky.

JUST ABOUT TO HAVE A MASSAGE!

SHE MESSAGES ME THIS.

. . .

SUPREMELY JEALOUS. *Stop texting me and enjoy yourself, you nutter.*

THAT'S MY REPLY, and then I put my phone face-down on the table in front of me. I don't want her to give me a running commentary of her amazing day; I'm envious enough as it is.

She's a lucky girl to have King. And he's the luckiest guy in the world to have her.

I settle back into the sofa and bring the tea up to my lips when the doorbell rings.

Great. *Perfect* timing.

I sigh and place my mug on the coaster next to my phone as the doorbell rings again.

Jeez.

"I'm coming, I'm coming."

Hold on. Could it be the murderer?

Do murderers even ring doorbells before they kill you?

Grace, you've been watching too many crime shows. You're paranoid.

I open the front door to a delivery man and not a murderer. He makes me sign for a package.

"Just the one?" I ask.

The delivery man shakes his head and gestures behind him at five giant parcels.

"What? All of those?"

"Yep."

"I didn't order anything."

It must be for Scarlett, but surely, she would've warned me that she's ordered a bunch of stuff.

"Your name's written down here," the delivery man says, showing me the words. He's right.

"Okay. Thanks."

Rick, the fish and chip shop owner from downstairs, pokes his head around.

"Everyfink okay, Grace?" he asks in his thick Cockney accent.

"All good, Rick."

He eyes the delivery man suspiciously before slinking back around into his shop.

That man is determined to look after me. It's very sweet.

When the delivery man leaves, I carry the heavy boxes one-by-one up the stairs into my flat, cursing whoever sent me these. But I'm also super curious as to what they contain.

I really didn't order this stuff, so who the hell did?

When the last box is safely in my living room, I sigh again and stumble over to the sofa, exhausted.

Well, I guess that was my gym session sorted for the year.

I'm not even bothered to open the boxes yet. I need a minute to breathe first. But before I do, on the table in front of me, my phone buzzes.

Probably Scarlett again. Deliberately rubbing in how nice her spa day is. I quickly check the phone.

But it's not her. It's Duke.

GOT MY PACKAGES YET?

OH, the little shit.

YEP. *So. You're the bastard I have to blame. Thanks for making me carry them all up the stairs.*

. . .

I WILL KILL HIM; I swear to God.

HOLD ON TIGHT, *Grace. I'm coming round.*

GREAT. Absolutely no way.

LIKE HELL YOU ARE.

HE DOESN'T MESSAGE me back, but that is no sign that he's not coming. I know well enough that nothing can stop a Heath-Harding boy.

He's definitely coming around.

DUKE RINGS my doorbell not long later. I don't even have time to apply my makeup or tidy up my messy hair. I open the door to him, my arms crossed and feeling damn self-conscious about my looks.

"I haven't opened those bloody parcels yet because I'm going to give them straight back to you," I say to the man smirking in my doorway.

"No, you're not."

"As I said in my message, I had to carry them all up the stairs. Thanks again for that."

"Well done," he replies. "You want a medal?"

"You're so infuriating, Duke."

If he's disgusted by my no-makeup and crazy-hair

appearance, it does not show in his face at all. He doesn't care. In fact, he looks at me like he can devour me now. Like he wants to rip my dressing gown off right here and fuck my body into oblivion.

Well, not just yet, mister. I want to tell him. *Don't stare at me like that. Take your rubbish away before I even contemplate having your perfect naked body near mine.*

"Now you have to carry them down yourself, Duke. I'm not helping you."

"I'm not going to take them anywhere. They're living here. Let's unpack them."

He dashes up the stairs before I could say anything. I follow him up, fuming. He's already slicing open one parcel with his keys when I reach the living room.

"Forget about it, Duke."

"You're going to at least see what I've sent you before you get all moody?" he asks.

"*Moody?*"

"Come on, have a look."

Begrudgingly, I do. I lean over his shoulder to see inside the open package. I am curious as to what he's sent, although I will never reveal that to him.

It's a box full of notebooks.

"What is it?" I ask.

He pulls them out and holds them aloft in the air like they're a prize. "My notes on the murderer so far. Well, it's mostly my notes and also a compilation of the police files on the case. All the information we have on the guy."

I have a sharp intake of breath. Now this has piqued my interest.

"What's in the other boxes?" I ask, gesturing to the ones scattered around my living room. Cluttering up my space.

Duke grins broadly like it's fucking Christmas and he's Santa. A bloody sexy Santa. "I've got you a computer."

"A what?"

"A state-of-the-art desktop computer for you to sort through all these notes and catch this guy. I should have a lot of programs installed on there. Police records. Databases. The lot. Everything and anything to nail the bastard."

I shouldn't let this man bribe me into his bed by buying me stuff, but *damn*, this is real impressive.

"Hm."

Duke sees straight through my pitiful attempt to hide my excitement.

"I want us to be a team," he says. "Let's get him together and make sure King and Scarlett's wedding all goes ahead. Let's put this guy behind bars so that we can live the rest of our lives in peace. Will you do that, Grace? Will you help me?"

I take in another breath. The look on his face. So expectant. So enthusiastic. He's like a little boy.

And he wants me.

"Okay," I reply.

"Just one favor to ask from you," he says, raising a finger. "Something I need you to do for me in return."

"What now?"

Duke steps towards me.

"Well, I've figured out what you want. Like you said in Harrods."

I raise an eyebrow.

"Oh, yeah? What is it?"

He takes another step towards me. I breathe him in and I can't control how much my body is trembling at his proximity.

"I know you, Grace. You're an impulsive girl and I've got just the thing for you. Exactly what you want. I'll leave you to unpack all this stuff and then I want you to come round my place tonight. Midnight. You remember where I live?"

"Yep. I remember. Why do you want me to come around tonight?"

He doesn't answer my question. Instead, he just smiles.

"I'll see you at midnight, Grace."

29

DUKE

GRACE TURNS up at exactly midnight, just as I told her to do. I smile when I open the door and see her standing there, ready for me. Despite all her sassiness, her coming here when I tell her to means that she does have a soft spot for me. I guess she really can't resist me.

"Hello," she says in my doorway. All cute and fuming.

Yes, that's the Grace I've fallen for.

"Hi."

In a nice dress with heels, Grace is definitely not dressed for what I've got planned, but that's the whole idea. I'm going to surprise her, and I think she'll like it.

"I think you're going to want to take those heels off," I say to her, eyeing her shoes.

Grace narrows her eyes at me suspiciously.

"What do you mean?"

"Here, take these."

I reach behind me into my hallway. I've got a pair of flats that are about her size. I hand them over to her.

"Where did you get these from?" Grace asks as she takes them from me and measures them against her feet. "One of your many trophies from girls who've slept here with you?"

"Something like that."

She grunts at my joke and slides the flats on. They fit.

Good.

"Follow me," I instruct her as I brush past her, shutting the door behind me. Grace folds her arms across her chest and pouts at me. It's real cute when she does that. She thought she'll be coming to my flat to do something fancy and nice.

Well, just the opposite.

"Where are we going, Duke?" she asks.

I say nothing. I just take her hand in mine and gently tug her along back down the street where she came.

All around us is silence. The houses are still. Night has fallen. London is dark.

I lead her a few streets away from mine to the edge of the park. It's not far.

"Hampstead Heath?" Grace raises an eyebrow as she realizes where we're going, not very impressed. "And what exactly are we doing here at night?"

"We're going in," I reply, smirking.

"*What?* But it's night, and it's closed."

But I've already opened the gate and stepped inside the dark park. I pull Grace in alongside me. She mumbles something incoherent, probably something about how much of a dick I am. Oh, I love it.

"I can't see. I better not fall over," she whispers. "If I do, I'm blaming you for eternity."

"Don't worry, I'll hold on to you."

"You better not let anything happen to me, Duke."

"Like what?"

"Like get eaten by a fox or something."

"A fox?" I laugh. "Trust me, no fox is coming to get you tonight. I'll bat them off if they try."

"Oh, you really are *my savior*," she mocks.

"Come on, Grace. Hurry up and follow me."

We head inside the park in the darkness. There are no lights, and so no way to see where we're going, but I know exactly where I want to take the girl.

I know Grace is worried about the darkness, even if she tries to hide it. She lifts her chin up and strolls alongside me to pretend she's brave, but I delicately wrap a protective arm around her, and she starts to lean on my shoulder.

That's my girl.

She doesn't have to pretend anything with me. I see through her armor. I want her to be that sweet young shop assistant who told me there's no way I could play the Didgeridoo and who stalked me to a jazz nightclub to watch me play. I want to rewind the years and relive that night again and get her to never leave.

I want Grace Madden all to myself for the rest of time.

"How much further?" she asks into my chest.

"Not far."

"Okay..."

Her voice is full of trepidation. I mean, she does have every right to be worried. We *are* going into a dark and scary park at night with absolutely no idea of what we're about to do.

I take her to a large fence that rings around a bit of the inside of the park. Grace looks up at me, confused.

"We're sneaking through," I say, nodding at the fence.

"How, Duke? I don't want to ruin my dress. Have you even thought of that?"

I immediately lean over and pick her up completely off the ground. Grace squeals in surprise as she's lifted into the air, but I know she likes it. I lift her over the tip of the fence with all my strength and gently lower her on the other side until her feet can touch the ground.

Then I leap over the fence.

"Duke! What was that for?"

Grace stares at me in indignation.

I pull out my phone's torch and shine it over her dress.

"See? Not a stain in sight. Nothing's ruined."

She slaps me playfully on the arm.

"Don't you dare pick me up like that again."

"Come on, you loved it. You *love* how strong I am. And, hey, even if your dress got ruined, I'll just get you a new one."

"That's not the point, Duke."

"Hey, you wanna see why I've brought you here or not?"

She crosses her arms and glares at me. "Okay. Show me."

She might be angry, but she is still curious.

We stagger through a bush and end up in front of a large body of water.

"Hampstead Ponds," Grace gasps. "No way."

"Exactly."

"I've never been," she whispers. "I've always wanted to go."

"I thought that'll be the case."

Grace looks up at me. "But I don't have any swimmers. How can I go in there? Certainly not in my dress."

"There's no one else around," I reply before I pull down my jeans.

And... I'm naked.

Grace giggles at the sight of me.

"Don't laugh, Grace. This is nothing you haven't seen

before." I raise my arms. "You said you wanted something impulsive. Well, here you go."

She covers her mouth and continues to laugh.

"You're crazy, Duke. You really are."

"You love it."

"I don't know why I put up with you."

"Stop dithering and follow me. Now it's your turn to strip down, Grace."

She shakes her head defiantly. "Nope. No way."

"Come on, I'll help you."

She smiles and spins around so that I can access the back of her dress. I slowly remove each button until the dress just slides off from her bare shoulders. Her milky skin is cold in the nighttime air. I run my fingers along her neck. She shudders at my touch. I lean down carefully and begin to kiss the edge of her collarbone.

Grace murmurs my name.

"Duke..."

It's so tempting just to bring my head back up and kiss her on the lips, but I stop myself.

I'm here to seduce her and I've got all night to make her come into my arms. There's no need to rush a thing when I have until dawn to make her mine.

I look into her light blue eyes and run my hand through her thick black hair.

"You're right," she whispers. "Screw you, Duke. You're right. This *is* what I want."

I don't know if she's talking about me undressing her or the Ponds.

I take her hand again and lead her to the edge of the deep water. I turn to her.

"Let's go in."

"I don't know..."

"We'll dive in," I command her sternly. "Together."

30

GRACE

WE RUN.

Through the dark park, back towards the gate we came in from.

"I can't believe we're doing this," I squeal at Duke as we sprint, fully naked, through Hampstead Heath. We're both wet and shivering cold from the Ponds. Despite my initial trepidation of the night and the water, it was fun to swim in the dark. Just us two and that deep body of water. Duke had made me feel so safe. He took my hand before we dived in and never let go. With the burly man swimming by my side, I felt like I could conquer the world. I felt like I could swim anywhere with him. But now we need to get back and dry ourselves off before we freeze to death.

I grip my lovely dress to my boobs, trying hard not to think of how much I might be damaging it as we make our way back through the muddy park.

Duke's smile gleams at me in the moonlight.

"That's Parliament Hill," he shouts to me as we run,

pointing up to a hill in the park that overlooks London. "The best view of the city's up there."

"Nice."

"Maybe we should go up there sometime."

We giggle like naughty schoolchildren as we make it to the streets. I wrap my poor dress around me to try to provide some sort of modesty as we pass houses, but Duke doesn't care at all about what he looks like. He's completely exposed and doesn't give a fuck. The man is so cocky.

This feels so wrong.

But also, so goddamn right.

I would never have done something like this with someone else, but Duke's confidence is infectious. He's fun in a way I've never seen from another guy. He makes me feel like I can do anything with him next to me.

And at least he doesn't live far.

I should be angry at him for taking me to the Ponds in the first place and getting me all wet and dirty, especially when I was wearing that nice dress. But I simply can't stay mad at that sexy face. I must admit that swimming in the Ponds was a hella lot of fun.

We rush through his building, not stopping until we shut his front door. My lips tremble; that's how cold I am. I bet they are blue.

I laugh through my breathlessness. My lungs are gasping for air like I've run a marathon. We both laugh at how stupid that was.

"Insanely stupid," I say, and Duke nods.

"What were we thinking?"

"You were the one who came up with the idea of skinny dipping in the Ponds. You just never thought about how cold it was going to be."

"It was worth it, though."

"Definitely."

"And you loved it," Duke replies. I have to agree.

Damn, it was bloody awesome swimming like that. It was so *naughty*. So secretive. No one is allowed at the Ponds after they close at night, but Duke broke us in. And I really did love it.

"Absolute *criminal* behavior," I say. Duke laughs.

"I am a bad boy."

Duke disappears into the bathroom and quickly returns, throwing a fresh towel at me. I take it and dry myself off. Heat slowly returns to my body.

Our laughter slows, and a silence falls over us. I lower my towel as Duke steps towards me, his big hands finding my arms. I can't stop thinking of the fact that we're both fully naked. His firm muscles drip with water. It glistens on his skin. I have a sudden temptation to put my cold lips on his. He looks at me with a gleam in his eyes.

He wants me, I know.

"Is this okay?" he asks me as his fingers dance across my arm.

"More than okay."

I know I shouldn't be giving in to him like this, but I simply can't resist.

The man owns me.

"You remember at Harrods?" I ask him, my voice trembling from both cold and restrained desire. "You remember when I said that you need to find out what I want?"

Duke shuffles even closer, his hot breath warming my face. I bite my lower lip, feeling a sigh of longing for him ready to burst out.

"Yeah."

"Well, this is what I want," I reply. "Running naked through Hampstead Heath. Something that means freedom, liberation. Something wild with you."

"I thought it would be," Duke whispers. "That's what I want too."

His arms wrap tight around me. His biceps tense up and I feel engulfed by him.

And then, just as I want to happen, his lips find mine.

Almost immediately, I pull away. Not much, but just enough to make Duke furrow his eyebrows and groan at my retreat from his lips.

"You really are insufferable, Grace."

"Well, then. If I'm so *insufferable* to such a big and powerful man, then you have just got to punish me for it, don't you think?"

I'm so cheeky.

He snarls at me, and I know for sure that my wish is going to come true.

I sneak a glance down at his naked body that's presented before me in all its splendor. His erect cock stands ready. Thick and veiny and massive. He's ready for my mouth or my pussy. It's just as I remember.

Oh God, it's just like my wild dreams.

No one has ever made me feel this sexy before. No one has made me feel so fucking *wanted.*

"You need to be punished?"

I nod. "I've been such a bad little girl."

"I can see that."

With my suggestion of discipline, Duke's hands quickly and desperately grab me, and I feel his massive erection press against my leg.

My pussy trembles.

"Oh, I very much intend to punish you," Duke seethes quietly into my ear.

If I wasn't turned on before, then I certainly am now.

I want to say to him *do with me what you want.* Take me in any way you choose. Don't let me say no.

"Duke…"

Just saying his name lights a fire in the man.

He pulls me in for another kiss. This time, I cannot object to his advances. This is the kiss of a man taking what he wants.

Me.

I taste his lust for me. I feel it as he holds my body tight and forcefully takes my mouth with his.

I knew precisely when we entered the place where this is leading us, and this is something I have been fantasizing about for days.

If not years.

I am surrendering to him inch by inch. There's no going back now.

"I want to be good," I whisper as our lips part.

"You're not good for me, Grace."

In a moment of unrestrained desire, I reach down for his exposed cock. My hands find the thick head and my body shivers in full surrender to him. I start to jerk him off. I'm so fucking wet.

"Let me show you how good I can be," I reply.

I bend down on my knees in front of his groin and immediately take his manhood in my mouth. Duke grunts. It's so freaking good to make this tall, strong man succumb to just the feel of my wet lips. My hands grip his buttocks as Duke tilts his head back and inhales. His fingers wrap around the back of my neck.

"Grace," he moans. "*Grace.*"

I pull myself off him.

"What, Duke?"

I look up at him, smiling mischievously. I've stopped, and he certainly doesn't like it.

"Keep doing what you're doing, Grace. Keep doing it."

And that's when I let go of his cock in direct violation of his commands.

"Nope."

Punish me.

My teasing has gone too far, judging by the look on Duke's face. He takes my chin and guides me up to my feet angrily. I like that glimpse of temper in his eyes. Duke takes a moment to soak me in, his eyes flickering over my naked body. I have never felt so naked in my life.

Or so desired...

"Now you need to really be punished," he says.

I gulp out of both fear and also delightful anticipation.

"The truth is that I'm not a good girl," I whisper. "The truth is that I *want* to be punished."

Duke leads me to his room with a force from him that I've been dying to witness. He pushes me face down on his massive soft bed. He holds both my hands back with one of his. I hear him unwrapping a condom behind me before he speaks into my ear.

"You want me to do this?"

"Yep."

"You're such a little slut for me."

"I am, Duke. I am."

"I'm going to ride you hard as your punishment because I have to, but let me assure you, Grace, that I'm going to enjoy every second."

Oh. So am I.

That's what I want to say to him, but my mouth is muffled by his bedsheets. I would love to provoke him even more - I would love to see what he would dare do to me if I did – but right now I'm too restrained by his powerful hold to even protest.

And it's just the way I like it.

"I'm going to punish you like the bad little girl you are,"

Duke mutters. I nod enthusiastically into his silk sheets. He doesn't let go of my hands pinned behind my back. "So bad for me."

And then, in one dominant thrust, he enters me. My eyes roll into the back of my head. I gulp.

He fucks me hard from behind, not holding anything back. His grunting grows louder and louder with each thrust.

"Duke..."

When I moan his name, he pushes in me even deeper and harder than before. I swallow, holding back tears of bliss from the pressure of his massive cock.

I feel so full. Of him.

His spare hand dances around my burning, wet pussy until he discovers my clit. His touch on the center of my pleasure makes my body shake. He pinches my clit between his fingers, making me moan again with uncontrollable delight.

I want to break free from his grip so that I can trace my fingers across his face. Across his perfect jaw. I want to feel the man who's making me feel these things, but he's got me tied down to the bed like a dirty whore.

And I love it. I love how he's treating me.

"You're all mine, aren't you?" Duke quietly asks me. It's a statement of fact rather than a question. "Don't even try lying. Your body is simply giving you away."

"Duke, fuck me like the bad boy you claim to be and then I'll decide whether or not I'm yours," I growl back.

Duke, just as I desire, takes that growl as a challenge. He roars like a beast and fucks me even harder. I'm crushed below his thick legs and muscular hips.

This is exactly the way I want.

He continues to tease my clit. His fingers play with me effortlessly, and I fall under his spell.

Hot damn.

"Duke..."

I moan again.

"Duke..."

His body quivers. I can feel he's about to come and it's driving me crazy.

"Duke."

He lets go of my hands and slumps forward into me as he releases, and then it's him who's saying *my* name.

"Grace..."

He's all soft and tender now. A sharp contrast to the rough beast just a few moments ago. A rare vulnerable moment from the man. He's only letting *me* see this side of him, and it's only for a fleeting glimpse.

"Oh, Grace..."

And then he's strong again. He flips my body over in one go so that I'm facing him now.

And then he kisses me.

Deeply.

31

GRACE

Stroking my finger around Duke's chest, I listen to his heartbeat and stare out of his bedroom's open window. The sun's rising. It's morning in London.

He drifts in and out of sleep next to me, occasionally running his hand through my hair as I press my cheek against his muscular shoulder.

"I was wrong about you," I whisper.

Duke's awake to hear my comment. But only just.

"What do you mean?" he asks softly.

"I thought you were a dick, but it turns out you're really not. In the last few days, you've affected me in ways I never thought you could. In ways I never thought any man could."

I'm letting my guard down now. I'm opening myself up to him. Making myself vulnerable in the same way as when he showed me Audrey and her kids.

Whatever we have - whatever Duke and I are *going* to have - needs to start from a place of honesty. And I want him to know how much he's made me think in the last few days together. He really has affected me. He's hit me like an arrow straight on target.

"Affected you in a good or bad way?"

I raise my head up to meet his gaze. He's fully awake now. I like to see that flicker of doubt in him. It makes me know that he really wants me. He's scared of me running away from him.

"In a *very* good way," I answer back before I kiss his soft, full lips.

"Good."

I kiss him again. I really can't resist.

"Yep."

He checks his Rolex.

"You better have a shower, Grace," he says.

"Now?"

"Yes."

"Why?"

The flicker of doubt behind his eyes is gone, replaced by the steel look I've come to both hate and lust after.

"Just have a shower, girl."

"You're not kicking me out, are you?" I pretend to laugh, but I am secretly scared that might be the case. That despite all the care he's shown me, that maybe I am still just another object for Duke Heath-Harding to conquer.

He lifts us both up as he shuffles out of bed.

He offers me a hand.

"Come with me. I'll show you my bathroom."

I take it and follow him to the other side of his massive bedroom. His bathroom is just an en-suite, but it's much larger than any other private bathrooms I've seen. I mean, even his shower is, like, the size of my flat's entire bathroom. It's insane.

"Wow."

I immediately forget any fears of Duke kicking me out when I see how impressive this shower is.

It's so goddamn luxurious.

Duke chuckles at my reaction.

"I'll be here when you come out. You'll find everything you'll need in here. There are spare clean towels in those drawers." He points underneath the wide sink. "Have a good shower. Take your time."

Then he closes the door, leaving me alone in the bathroom.

I treat myself to a long shower. How could I not? The products the man has in here are top of the range stuff. If I doubted he was rich before, then I certainly don't now.

I wrap one of his many clean spare towels around me and head back on out to his bedroom, expecting to see him standing there waiting for me.

But he's not.

Instead, there's someone else there.

An older woman. In his bedroom. Her back is turned to me.

"Uh, hello."

She spins around, her lips pursed. She's immaculate. Perfect makeup and an amazing body for her age.

"Hello. Sorry to startle you," she says. She has an incredibly posh and clipped accent. Even colder than Duke's.

I suddenly feel very naked in front of her. It's just a towel covering my wet body. The woman's eyes glaze over me. I can't tell what she's thinking at all.

"Sorry," I reply. The most British response ever.

"Oh, you don't know who I am," the woman says. A smile dances across her face. "I'm Camilla. Duke's nanny."

Nanny? What the hell?

"Where's Duke?" I ask, stuttering in shock.

"He's around."

"Okay..."

"You must be the girl who broke his heart," she says.

Wow, she's blunt.

But, yeah, she's talking about me.

"Yeah, I'm Grace."

I hold my head up high. If this woman – this *nanny* – is gearing up for a fight, then she's going to get one. She takes a step towards me, staring at me with an inquisitive look.

"You know, Duke has an armor of steel around him at all times," she says. "Or, at least, he *pretends* to. Not many people have ever seen the real side of him; he doesn't open up enough to let them in. But you have. You're the girl whose disappearance made a sizable chink in Duke's defenses."

"What are you saying?" I ask, still not knowing where this weird conversation is going.

"I respect you," Camilla replies coolly. "I've been wanting to meet you for a very long time."

"Well, here I am."

"Yes," she says with a smile. "Here you are. The girl who really hit Duke hard. It's good to meet you finally."

I still have absolutely no clue who she is.

Suddenly, the bedroom door swings open to the side of us, and in walks both Scarlett and Kingsley.

I turn to them in shock.

"What are you guys doing here?"

Scarlett laughs at me.

"Why are you laughing?" I demand.

She covers her mouth.

"Oops, sorry. It's just so funny seeing you so annoyed. And nearly naked."

King rolls his eyes.

"Of course I'm annoyed. I've just walked into Duke's

bedroom practically naked with the three of you here," I say, hoping to make the strangeness of the situation come across to everyone.

Camilla doesn't say a word during all of this, she just stares at me as if she's sizing me up.

I really don't understand why she's said she's Duke's nanny, but if Scarlett doesn't seem to mind her, then I guess she's someone I have to accept.

But I don't get why a fully grown man like Duke needs a nanny.

"Well, Duke did tell us all yesterday that you'll be spending the night here," Scarlett says.

"Did he now?" I ask, my voice rising. "What a cheeky bastard."

Behind Scarlett and Kingsley, in walks Duke.

Finally. There he is.

The first thing he does is wink at me. That super sexy wink.

"You mentioned me?" he asks. He doesn't seem to be affected by the sudden crowd that's appeared in his bedroom, nor the girl he slept with last night being naked in front of them.

I hold the towel close to my chest.

"Why is everyone here?" I ask him, indignant.

"Well, it's Sunday," Duke says calmly, as if that explains all. "So, we're having Camilla's famous Sunday roast."

32

GRACE

WITH EVERYONE in another part of his penthouse, I turn to speak to Duke in private.

"Right, so she *was* your nanny?"

Duke looks at me like I've gone insane.

"Yeah, of course she was. When I was growing up," he replies. "Wait... are you telling me you thought she still *is* my nanny? What?"

I shrug, embarrassed. "Well, she did tell me she is your nanny."

Duke rolls his eyes and sighs. "Camilla loves saying that to annoy King and me."

"It's funny."

"No, it's infuriating. I better give her a good talking to."

I bite my lip, trying not to giggle. I get it now. "Come on, Duke. There's no shame in admitting you still need a nanny at your age."

"Hey now."

"You don't have to pretend you're a big boy," I tease, flashing him a smile. "I'm sure you still need someone to wipe your ass for you."

Duke glowers back at me.

"She doesn't wipe my ass."

"She once did, though, right?"

"A long time ago, Grace. When I was nappies."

"And you still keep her employed?" I ask.

"She looks after our family's country estate now. She's like a mother to King and me. We love her. We could never let her go, and she likes to work. So, she's stayed with us."

"Well, that's sweet."

It's just us two in his bedroom now. Camilla's in the kitchen putting the final finishes on the roast she's brought over, and King and Scarlett are getting the table ready in Duke's dining room. Thankfully, they've left me alone to get changed out of being naked and into something a little more respectable.

Duke's had a shower himself and is dressed in another one of his snazzy suits. I pull on his tie and bring him towards the bed.

I want to climb him like a tree.

"I can't resist you when you wear something so tight and cool," I whisper to him, my eyes darting down over his suit. His chest muscles are defined even through the shirt. "How about I rough you up a little before we go and eat? Make you truly hungry..."

Duke chuckles and gently pushes me away from his tie.

"Oh, Grace. I'm so hungry for you, but I've been waiting for this roast all week. You'll have to be dessert, I'm afraid."

I reach up and wrap my arms around the neck of the tall man and kiss his soft lips.

"I'm happy being a dessert," I whisper.

"You're sweet enough to be," Duke replies. He takes my hand in his and guides me towards the closed door. "Ready to meet the family?"

I exhale. "Yep. Let's do this."

* * *

"This roast is amazing," I exclaim as a bit of gravy dribbles down my chin. "It's so delicious, thank you, Camilla."

Duke and King's nanny gives me a cheeky wink.

"No problem, Grace."

Duke reaches over and dabs the trail of gravy on my face away with the back of his finger.

"See? I told you it's famous," he says.

"Oh, I don't doubt it is. No wonder Duke and King grew up so big and strong when this is the quality of food you fed them, Camilla."

She laughs.

The former nanny can really cook. I can see why the boys love her.

Scarlett takes one look at me across the table and bursts out laughing.

"You're still amused over earlier?" I ask her with one eyebrow raised.

"I'm sorry, Grace, but seeing you half-naked next to Camilla is a pretty damn funny sight."

I roll my eyes. "I hope karma bites you in the ass."

"We'll see," she replies. "At least you're fully dressed now."

"Yep. At least."

"I don't know about you," Duke chirps in as he takes a bite of beef. "But I found that sight to be pretty sexy."

"Ew," King moans.

"Now, boys and girls," Camilla interrupts with a firm tone. "No dirty talk at the table."

"Okay, Camilla."

"We're respectable," she continues. "Be proper gentlemen."

I glance at Duke and snigger. "She's *still* your nanny, big boy," I say. "She has you by the balls."

He glares at me, which only makes me snigger more.

Camilla slyly smiles.

"This has been a lovely afternoon," she says. "I should drop in more often."

"Hopefully when people are in a few more clothes," adds Scarlett. I poke my tongue out at her in response.

"You boys better finish everything on your plate," Camilla says, eyeballing them from across the table.

"Of course. We would never leave anything you cook untouched, Camilla," King replies. "You know that."

"Yeah," Duke chips in.

"Do I get a *thank you* for cooking all this?"

"We can do more than a *thank you*," King says, motioning Duke to stand up.

"What?" Camilla asks, concerned, as the two boys approach her with wicked smiles on their faces.

They both start kissing her cheeks jokingly.

Camilla emits a giggle I never expected from someone as ice-cold as her. "Alright, boys. Stop. *Please.*"

Duke and King back away from her face, laughing at how much she's blushing.

"Got you," King says.

Camilla wipes the spit from the kisses on her cheeks. "I hate it when you two do that."

"Boys." Scarlett looks at me and shakes her head. "I need to go to the restroom. Wanna join?"

"Sure."

We leave the boys and Camilla to continue bickering with each other and head into Duke's bathroom. Scarlett shuts the door and reapplies lipstick in the mirror as I sit on the edge of the bathtub and watch her.

"So... *last night...*" she mutters conspiratorially.

Oh, boy. I knew this was coming.

"What?"

Scarlett stares at me through the reflection.

"Go on. Tell me what happened."

"Nope."

I can't help myself but giggle. It's hard to keep anything from my best friend.

"Right. So *that* happened."

"My lips are sealed. A lady never tells."

"Wow, so things are progressing very fast," Scarlett says, sensing what's up.

I nod. "Yep, they seem to be."

"You hated him a few days ago."

"Oh, I certainly did."

"So... you like him?"

I take in a long breath.

"Maybe."

Scarlett lowers her lipstick. "Wow. Who'd ever see that coming? Grace Madden actually *liking* a boy."

"Crazy, right?"

After Scarlett finishes reapplying her makeup, we head back to the dining room. The boys have calmed down considerably and are starting to pack up the plates. I offer to take a plate from King, but Scarlett interrupts me.

"Don't worry, we'll do the washing up," she says. "You and Duke just chill, okay?"

As she says that, Duke takes my hand and leads me away from the table.

"I need to show you something," he says to me quietly.

"What?"

"In the bedroom." And then he lowers his mouth to my ear and whispers. "I want my dessert."

And I know *exactly* what he means.

33

DUKE

I ʟᴏᴠᴇ how Grace follows me into my bedroom like a little sex kitten the moment I whisper in her ear that I have to show her something.

She giggles in excited anticipation as I pull her into me and close the door behind us.

"We have to be quiet," I say to her. "We can't have anyone else hear us."

"I know. We're being so naughty."

She nods, but she still can't stifle her nervous laughter. It's very cute.

"Quiet, Grace. If you keep being loud, I'm just going to have to punish you," I say, hushed.

She likes that. She bites her lower lip and bass her eyelashes up at me.

Oh God, I simply can't get enough of this girl.

"I really do think you need to punish me," she replies sultrily. "Otherwise, I'm going to be *so* loud."

Fuck. Me.

"Oh, just you wait. I'll give you something to be loud about," I retort as I spank her ass. Grace whimpers. There's a thrill in her moan.

Fuck, she turns me on so fucking much.

I spank her again. Another sexy whimper from Grace.

I rip off her clothes. She helps worm free from what she's wearing. She's eager for me, that's for sure. Her naked body makes me shudder. My cock pushes up against my pants, erect.

"I can't believe we're doing this when everyone's in the other room," she says. "It turns me on so much."

"Be quiet, girl."

"You want me to be silent?"

"Yes."

"Make me."

"If you don't be quiet, then you won't get your treat."

Her mouth widens. "Treat?"

I lean into her ear. "If you don't shut the hell up, Grace, then you won't get my cock. How about that?"

She moans again.

She really wants my cock.

I can't hold myself back anymore. I must have her. I grab her wrists and push her down onto the bed. She doesn't struggle against me. Her eyes are buzzing full of elation and a sensual frenzy for me as I keep her down on the sheets. I can't stand it. I must ravish her. I must penetrate her and fill her up with my cock. I must dominate this gorgeous little sex kitten before she gets the better of me.

"Give yourself to me," I demand in a low voice.

"Duke..."

"Shh."

I raise a finger to her soft, wet lips to hush her. There's another whimper from deep within her. Grace squirms against my hold, but I keep her pinned down to her bed.

"You stay silent, you understand?"

"Mm."

"Good girl. It's time for your treat," I whisper.

"Yes, please."

With one hand, I undo my belt and pull out my massive cock. I'm so aroused that it's hard and glistening in pre-cum. Grace's eyes widen when she sees it. I love that look on her face.

That look is gonna kill me.

I enter her hard. She whimpers another time, and this drives me crazy. I push in so deep within her that I know she wants to squeal. I have her wrists pinned up above her head with my hands and I feel like I'm so in control. She's completely submitted herself to my power.

There's a danger of us doing this depraved act so close to my family. I see the mischievous gleam in Grace's eyes that tells me she's thinking the exact same thing.

"Oh, I like how we can be caught," I whisper in her ear. "This is so taboo."

"Yes."

"You're loving this, aren't you?"

Grace's body shudders under me. I feel her legs tremble against mine with titillation. She's close to climax, I know.

Her moans of pleasure are pushing me close to cumming as well. She doesn't know how much she has a stranglehold over me with every groan that escapes from her lips.

"Yes."

"You're a little slut, aren't you?"

Grace closes her eyes and nods. "I'm your little slut."

Shit. I can't handle this for long.

"That you are."

"I want you to cum inside me, Duke," she says. "Cum inside your little slut."

I push in deep.

Fuck.

I climax. Hard and long. My strokes erupt into a wave inside Grace. Her eyes roll into the back of her head as she's filled with me/

"Grace..."

I moan her name.

She kisses the side of my neck and I collapse in exhaustion.

We lie still for a moment before she speaks.

"You said you had to show me something in here," she says, breathless. "Well, I've got something to show you."

I bite my lip.

"What is it?"

"Oh, you'll see."

She leans over the side of the bed and reaches into her bag, pulling out something pink and small. The shape of an egg. I sit up when I see it.

Her vibrator.

Grace looks up from the device into my eyes and smiles a wicked smile.

"Duke, I want you to use this on me. Right now."

34

GRACE

"This is how I like it," I say to Duke as I guide him on how to use the vibrator against my wet pussy. He easily finds my clit and proceeds to play with it unprompted, sending overwhelming convulsions through my body as he controls my pleasure.

Fuck.

I fall back against his pillow and involuntarily arch my back, unable to regulate my movements at all. I'm so consumed by the waves of bliss that rock my core, all stemming from Duke's masterful handle on the buzzing device pressing against my sex.

The man knows how to bring me to the edge.

"Don't stop, Duke..."

He leans over me. In between bursts of pleasure, I open my eyes long enough to glance up at the muscular man. He's smiling at me.

That goddamn smile.

I know he's absolutely loving how powerful he's being.

He's loving how he can make my body shake with just a twist of the vibrator against my clit.

"Please don't stop. Never stop."

My lips part and I loudly sigh. Duke's hands reach for my mouth, and he gags me.

"No talking," he commands in a deep, authoritative voice. "Be quiet. I don't want the others to hear what I'm able to do to you."

I gulp.

So sexy.

I can't take him anymore. He's so goddamn big and strong and in control.

The heat from my pussy is stunning me. I climax not once, but twice.

And still Duke continues to press on the vibrator, making me moan and my body launch into another set of waves.

"You like that?" he asks, growling.

"Yep."

He's in total domination over my body. He knows *exactly* what he's doing. He forces when he needs to, and he teases when he pulls away. Duke watches me intensely with his irresistible blue eyes, and I find myself lost in a sea of delight.

I feel like his complete attention is on me. On my needs. His cock is hard from observing me. My hands grip the bedsheets and I flatten hard against the mattress. My body wants to spin out of control.

Bloody hell.

I've never experienced anything like this before.

There is no running away from this man.

He owns me. Completely.

35

GRACE

THE SUN IS COMING down over London. I have the most
perfect view of it sitting on the picnic rug at the top of
Parliament Hill, the same place Duke had pointed out the
other day as the best view in London. And now we're here.

And I think he's right. This really is some view.

"Enjoying this?" Duke asks me, calling up from down
the hill. He has two children climbing over his back.
Damien's kids. Anna and Jack. They're giggling as they
force the tall man down with their weight onto the grass.

"I'm enjoying watching you struggle," I call back with a
smile. The kids squeal in excitement.

"Hey, I'm not struggling." Duke whips around and
tackles the two screaming kids into the ground. They laugh
as he picks each one up into the air and throws them around
with all that manly strength of his. They're loving it.

And so am I.

Duke and I asked Audrey if we could take the kids on a
picnic this evening and then for a sleepover with us. She

agreed enthusiastically; eager to get the kids off her hands for a night. Duke drove up and collected them from their place whilst I pre-packed dinner.

We found the perfect spot on Parliament Hill and sat there eating whilst looking out over the perfect view.

The last few hours have made me feel what it's like to have a family. To have kids to care for. I've never thought about it deeply before, but my broody senses are starting to tingle.

And I couldn't get one thing out of my head. I couldn't stop thinking that this could be the life I might have with Duke.

"You'll make a good father," I say to the man when he comes back up the hill, panting from the exercise of playing with the kids. They continue to dart around in the grass whilst Duke takes a long sip of the cold beer I hand him.

"Don't even talk to me about that," he says, breathless.

"Aw, you sure you don't want one or two little Heath-Hardings running around?"

Duke lowers the beer bottle.

"Depends on who the mother is."

My heart pounds. He's looking at me as he says that.

Does that mean this thing we've got going might be a long-term thing?

What is this man thinking?

"What kind of mother are you looking for?" I ask him.

"Oh, someone kind. Nurturing. Helps a lot too if they're extremely hot."

"Well, I fit all of those boxes, especially the last one."

"Grace, I think so."

"Right, so you want me to be your girlfriend?" I ask teasingly. I play it lightly, but I'm also deadly serious.

Duke smiles at me before taking an impossibly long gulp of his beer.

And then he finally answers.

"It's pretty obvious."

Oh. Wow.

Before I can reply, Jack sprints up to the picnic rug and tugs on Duke's arm.

"Can we play catch?" he asks Duke.

"What's the magic word?"

"I dunno."

"Sure, you do. Ask me again."

"Can we play catch... *please?*"

"That's better."

The two scramble back down the hill with Duke gripping a ball. He turns and gives me a little wave. It's so cute that it makes my heart burst.

Damn. I've really fallen for this guy, haven't I?

And he wants me to be his girlfriend. I can't believe it.

I smile as he starts to throw the ball back and forth to Jack. I continue to watch them as the sun goes down over London, happy with my life.

Yep, this truly is a perfect spot for a picnic.

* * *

"No more bedtime stories," I whisper to Jack and Anna as they lie in bed.

"One more?" Jack asks cheekily.

I smile and shake my head. "You've had two from Duke and one from me already tonight. No more."

"Okay, then."

Before I turn off the light switch, I watch them for a moment. They're so adorable all tucked up in bed. Today has truly been one of the best days I've had for a long time. Picnic in the park followed by bedtime stories. This could be the life I might even have with Duke one day.

He would make a great father.

"Goodnight, you two."

"Goodnight, Miss Madden."

I chuckle and switch off the bedroom light before shutting the door.

"How are they?" Duke asks, whispering, as I enter our bedroom. He's stripping off for bed. He sleeps in only his underwear. I watch his thick biceps as he pulls down his pants.

"They want more bedtime stories."

"That's crazy," he replies. "They've already had three."

"I know."

"They're like hungry seagulls, always wanting more."

"They're so sweet though," I reply. "It's very hard to say no to them."

Duke sighs. "They've got me hook, line, and sinker. I love those two little scallywags."

He approaches me. I can already see the hard erection tenting up his pants.

"Come to bed," he whispers into my ear. His hands find the buttons on the back of my dress and he's already undoing them before I can answer.

"You're being naughty, Duke. The kids might hear us."

He kisses my neck slowly and gently. "Well, I guess we've had a lot of practice being quiet recently."

My mind casts back to the other day when he fucked my brains out whilst Camilla, King, and Scarlett were in the other room. Damn, that was proper naughty.

"I guess we're experts at fucking whilst keeping quiet."

Duke doesn't reply to that. He's too busy removing my bra whilst kissing down my collarbone to my exposed breasts. His mouth discovers my nipple, and he bites on it, sending heat through my body.

Damn, the boy can turn me on.

I moan as his fingers trace across my body.

"This is very bad of you, Duke," I whisper. "You're

making me very horny."

"Call me daddy," he demands.

"Oh, *daddy*, you're making it very hard to resist you."

"Then don't."

He pulls me to the bed.

This time it's different. He's no longer the unrestrained animal he's been; this time he's slow. Tender. Gentle.

He's making *love* to me.

Duke thrusts inside me and fucks me as he stares deep into my eyes. I lose myself in his sea of blue. A connection forms between us, unbreakable and enduring. This is beyond simple bodily pleasure. This is pure loving.

"Oh, daddy," I repeat as he pushes in deep. "Daddy."

We've made a bond together, and it feels like nothing can tear it apart.

* * *

AFTER SEX, we lie in bed together in dreamy silence. Duke's muscular arm is wrapped around me, making me feel so incredibly safe and comfy. I softly kiss his perfect bicep and lean my cheek against his smooth skin.

I want to stay here forever. I want to find my way inside this man's head and figure out what he's thinking at all times. I want to know this gorgeous man inside and out forever.

"So, do you want to be my girlfriend?" Duke asks quietly, breaking the silence.

My heart stops.

He never heard my answer in the park.

I twist my head to look at him in his blue eyes.

"I would like that very much," I reply.

Duke smiles.

And that's when I know he's mine.

36

DUKE

I'm sitting in my office at the top of my company's skyscraper. It's always hard to describe what exactly I do for a living. I tell people at parties that I essentially make a hell of a lot of money by owning a hell of a lot of companies. I invest. I buy. I sell. On an international scale.

That's what I do, and it's made me incredibly wealthier even on top of my ancestral wealth. The perks of owning my own companies and my considerable fortune are that I can spend it on things I want to spend it on. I only own ethical companies that are making the world a better place. I would rather forsake a good cheque than invest in something that ruins and destroys.

Leave the world a better place than when I came into it.

That's been my motto.

And maybe making a fuckload of money at the same time wouldn't hurt.

And today, it's another day in my office. Another day of making another pile of dough. I'm checking over the day's stock figures as I sit at my desk. My portfolio has been going from strength to strength this year thanks to some quick smart decisions I made earlier last year. It's a hard game I play, but when you do the right thing, then you can reap the dividend.

I'm about to finish reading the latest report when there's a knock on my door.

"Come in."

"Mr. Heath-Harding," says my secretary. She's got an envelope in her hand. "A letter has arrived for you. It's marked urgent."

I motion for her to bring it and leave it on my desk.

"That will be all, thanks."

I sit down in my chair, looking out over the view of London. Grace is down there somewhere, probably getting ready for her next tour group. That makes me smile. I've bought her tour company. Such a stupid thing to do, but I saw their figures. They were collapsing. At least now I can keep that business afloat and make sure that Grace can do the thing she loves.

I would do anything for that girl. I would spend all my money buying a million tour group companies if that made her happy.

She means the world to me.

And now she's my girlfriend. How lucky can one guy be?

A few days ago, I thought she was lost to me completely. The girl who disappeared four years ago. And now we're together.

Life doesn't get much better than that.

As I look out over my city, I absent-mindedly pick up the letter on my desk and prise it open.

I immediately recognize the handwriting enclosed within. I've seen those spidery, inky loops before.

I've seen them at the police station.

Fuck.

It's a letter from the killer.

In surprise, I drop the piece of paper onto my desk, not wanting my fingerprints to tamper with the evidence. I can still read the writing, though.

DEAR YOU SON OF A BITCH. *I am out to get you and your brother. Don't think I've disappeared. I've seen you living your best life. Well, that won't last for very long. I'm coming to destroy your world, Mister Duke.*

I DON'T REACT to the letter in any emotional way. My first thought turns to action. What I can do to fix this.

I pick up my phone and start to make some very important calls.

We need to nail this bastard, but first I've got to make sure my world is safe.

* * *

"I NEED you to pack up your computer equipment. Now."

"Why?"

Grace blinks at me, confused by what I'm saying. I know she's not going to do anything without an explanation. She's tough like that. My girl.

"I've just got another threat from the killer. A letter delivered straight to my office this time," I say as I stand in the doorway to her flat. I've just arrived and knocked on her door urgently. She has no clue why I'm here. "We need to get out of this flat straight away and to somewhere that's safe."

Grace pauses for a moment to take in the information and then nods. She's serious. She knows the severity of the situation. She's going to follow my instructions.

I help her get her computer stuff. We take it down the stairs of her flat into the back of my car.

Scarlett emerges from her bedroom, bleary-eyed from a nap. King isn't with her. I continue to pack my car with their belongings as Grace takes her into her room to explain what's happening. A moment later, they're both helping me without saying another word.

I'm coming to destroy your world...

Well, I'm not going to let that happen. I don't know how real that threat is. I don't know if the killer is heading here right now, but I want to get the girls to safety.

They're my world. Mine and King's. If the killer is out to destroy what we love, then Scarlett and Grace will be his number one target.

We finish packing quickly, and then we're locking up the girls' flat. Making sure no one can get in without a crazy amount of force.

We get in my car, and I drive us to King's apartment. They should be safe there. For now.

"What does he want?" Grace asks me. She sits on the back seat next to Scarlett, holding her hand. I'm proud of how strong the girls are being. They're calm. Focused. Ready.

"I don't know," I reply. "Probably money, I think."

"I don't think so," Grace says. "I don't think he's after money at all."

"What do you mean?"

"If he wanted money, he would've asked for it by now. Why else spend weeks tormenting us without a reward?"

"What do you think he wants, then?" I ask.

Grace shrugs. "He wants to be seen. He wants an audience. There's no way he's motivated by money if this is the way he's going about things. Kill someone in such a dramatic way and then spend weeks sending threatening letters? That's not the behavior of someone desperate for money. That's the behavior of a man who wants people to notice him."

I frown. She's right. Grace is so damn smart.

"I'm impressed," I say.

"I watch a lot of true crime documentaries," Grace replies.

We get to King's penthouse in short time. We unload the car and bring the bags upstairs. King and Scarlett go off into his bedroom to talk things over. Grace and I get the couch.

There's nothing to do now but to think through it all. See if there's any detail left unturned. We need to figure out our next steps. We need to get ahead of this asshole.

Grace and I sit on the couch in silence, gently rubbing each other's arms as a way of comforting ourselves.

"Promise me something, Duke," Grace says softly after a while.

"What is it?"

Her voice is faint. She's worried.

"Promise me that you'll include me in everything that you do."

I turn to her and stop running my fingers over her arm. "Why are you asking me this?"

"Scarlett got King to promise her something similar, and I think I need you to do the same. I don't want to be some rich man's accessory. I want to be his equal."

I nod. I understand what she's saying. I can see *why* she's saying it.

"You and I are equal, Grace. You wouldn't believe how

much I look up to you. We're partners in this. I promise I'll include you in everything."

And then Grace smiles. Despite all the pressure we're under, despite the threats, that smile lights up the entire room for me.

37

GRACE

I DON'T KNOW what's going to happen, and I'm scared.

I'm scared for Scarlett. I'm scared for King.

But, most of all, I'm scared for Duke.

After days of thinking they're invincible, he and King are finally taking the killer's threats seriously, and that's only because he's announced he's coming for their world.

Scarlett.

Me.

I only hope Duke doesn't do anything stupid. I especially hope that he actually includes me in his plans, like he promised.

He better because there would be hell to pay if he doesn't. I'll see to that.

"We'll be safe here," Duke says, trying to reassure me about King's penthouse as we sit on King's couch. But I don't need the man's empty words. He knows as much as I do about how safe we are. Which is *not at all*.

"We're still in London," I reply. "We're still within reach of the killer. You think he doesn't know the address of King's apartment? You think a guy like this has not got plans or hasn't researched? He's already killed once, he's able to kill again."

Duke purses his lips, thinking hard. I reach over and take his hand.

"As long as we're together," I say. We both don't know what to do.

"Yeah, as long as we have each other."

The door to King's bedroom opens and in walks Scarlett. She's all wet still from just having had a shower. She was napping when Duke decided to burst into our flat and tell us about the threat he'd received, so she hasn't had time to properly wake up from it. Poor her, she's more disorientated than we are.

King follows behind her.

"You two okay?" Scarlett asks.

Duke and I nod.

"How are you guys?" Duke asks his brother and Scarlett.

"Pretty shaken, but okay," King replies.

Scarlett sits down next to us on the couch. "We're going to have to deal with this."

"This whole thing is pretty scary," I say.

"Yeah, I feel it too," Scarlett replies. "What are we going to do?"

"Well, I'm not just going to sit around here doing fuck all and waiting for this guy to show up," I say, prizing open a box containing my computer. "Now is the time to finally sit down, research, and get this bastard."

Scarlett shuffles over close to me and helps me pull the computer out.

The two boys stare at us. I'm guessing they're surprised by our abundance of steel and determination. They should know by now that Scarlett and I don't ever quit.

We start to set up the computer. Scarlett smiles at me.

"Yes, let's get him."

I KNEW where my victim was staying. I knew all about her whereabouts. I knew exactly how to get her.

It was not hard.

In fact, it was very easy.

They thought they were safe, staying where they're staying. They thought no one can touch them there.

Well, weren't they incredibly wrong...

I'm going to get them. I'm going to ruin their little world.

By this point, I had thought about my plan for days. Formulating it up in my mind. All the ways I could do that. I scouted out where they were staying. I knew the entrances. The exits. Their movements. Routine.

Everything.

It was a foolproof plan, and I was going to execute it with my superior ability. No one could stop me now.

I went where I knew I needed to go. In the dead of night. When I knew they'll be asleep. When they'll be most vulnerable.

I jumped the security. I smashed through the window. I left no trace of me behind. No one would know it was me, just like how they didn't know it was me who got that stupid little Ben Helper man. The police didn't even have one clue about me.

It was almost too easy to even be a challenge. It was almost boring.

But on I went. And I reached their bedroom. I saw their body asleep under their sheets.

It was them. Lying right there.

And I was going to get them.

Kidnap them.

The next step of my master plan.

Everything was coming together.

38

GRACE

WE SPEND the next few hours researching online. Looking at the similarities of the loopy handwriting of the man's. Looking for patterns in the killer's actions.

King and Duke spend a lot of the time in the other room on the phone with the police while this happens.

It's when it's really quiet - with both Scarlett and I intensely reading an article we've found on how to identify handwriting - when the doorbell rings. It makes us both jump in surprise.

"I'll get it," I say to Scarlett.

Surely it can't be the killer, can it?

I open the door to a delivery man. He makes me sign for a large package. Probably something addressed for King. It's big enough for me to have to carry it with both hands even though it's extremely light.

I take it inside, but then I realize that it's actually addressed to me.

For this address.

Grace Madden.

My heart drops, and I lower the box carefully on the dining room table, my hands shaking nervously.

"What is it?" Scarlett asks.

"Boys!"

I call out and both King and Duke come running into the room, expecting the worse.

Duke's eyes immediately dart over my body, making sure I'm okay. "What's wrong, Grace?"

I just point at the box. At my name written there.

"No one else should know I'm here," I say. "Right?"

Duke shakes his head. "Yeah."

"Then why is this addressed to me?"

"Shit," King whispers.

"I'm going to open it," I declare.

"No, Grace." Duke is so damn cautious. He's treating me like a piece of china, delicate and frail.

"I can handle this," I reply to the man. He frowns at me. "This is addressed to me, so I should be the one to open it. This is my decision."

Ignoring any retort my boyfriend could make, I turn and head into the kitchen, finding some gloves to protect my hands. I go back up to the package and cut away the tape with a knife. I cautiously open the box with everyone crowded around me, watching curiously and with trepidation.

Inside the massive box is a single piece of paper with only one line of writing on it.

I'M COMING to get you.

. . .

THE WHOLE ROOM falls silent as soon as we read what's written.

And then Duke speaks.

"We need to leave. Now."

* * *

"THE BEST PLACE I can think of is our family's country manor," Duke says in the car as we head out of London. The tall buildings of the city give way to green fields as the car zooms out on the fast lane on the motorway. "You guys will be safe there."

"How are you sure the killer doesn't know about the manor?" I ask from the backseat.

It's all of us in Kingsley's Aston Martin. Pretty goddamn cramped, especially with all the luggage we quickly packed away as soon as we received the latest threat. King is driving, of course. He never lets anyone else drive his beloved vehicle, even if there is an emergency.

And it certainly feels like we're in an emergency. Everyone is serious. No jokes. No smiles. No laughter.

The threats against our lives are becoming more and more real. It's like we're being slowly suffocated. The killer knows I was staying at King's.

Nowhere is safe.

Duke turns to me in his seat from upfront.

"I don't know, but it feels a hell of a lot safer for you than staying in London. There's more security at our manor. Camilla's there. There are groundskeepers. I just want to get you out of the city."

Next to me, Scarlett grips my hand tight. We've got each other.

No matter what.

"Remember you promised me that you'll treat me like an equal, Duke," I remind him. "Don't act like we're delicate princesses to be locked away safe in a tower."

His eyes lock with mine. "That's not what we're doing, Grace. I'm just making sure you are safe."

"Good. As long as we're on the same page."

"And that goes for us two as well, King," Scarlett repeats next to me. In the driver's seat, her fiancé nods in the mirror.

We arrive at the manor in a fairly short time. King drove incredibly fast that it's pretty surprising no police stopped him on the way.

Camilla is waiting outside the main doors with her trademark pursed lips and steely eyes. Duke was right, the place feels much safer than London. Secluded. Hard to find. I guess a famous family over the last few hundred years would make sure their ancestral home would be kept isolated from the outside world.

"Hopefully, the killer doesn't know about this place," I whisper to Scarlett. She frowns, clearly thinking the same thing.

Gentlemen as ever, even in times of crisis, Duke and King open our passenger doors.

"Hello, everyone," Camilla greets us.

The boys each give her a peck on the cheek.

"You got our message, then?" Duke asks her. Camilla nods somberly.

"This is a dreadful business. I've called some security guys I know. Former SAS types. They'll stay with us here tonight."

"How the hell do you know SAS guys?" King asks her.

"Oh, there's more to my life than just being your nanny, King."

"You *were* my nanny."

She guides us inside the main manor building. It's so impressive. I can see that this is a large estate. The grounds stretch on into the distance. There are marble columns ringing the manor house. In the main entrance of the mansion is an immense chandelier that I bet is worth a pretty penny or two. The place reminds me of a palace. On the walls hang portraits of ancestors staring imposingly down on visitors. There are so many artifacts decorating every room. I'm completely floored by the place.

We sit down and immediately Camilla goes to make us tea. Of course she does. It's the most British way to react to a problem.

Nothing a cup of tea can't fix.

"Don't worry," she says after she's returned from putting the kettle on. "You'll be safe here. Any intruder would have to get through me first and despite how old I may look; I've been around the block a few times."

She smiles at me. I know how rare that display of affection from the woman is. I smile back.

Even though it feels like we're on the run, I also feel a sense of family all around me.

King. Scarlett. Camilla. Duke. These people are my new family now. We can do anything together. Be safe together.

We just have to make sure we treat each other as equals.

We sit in comfortable silence for a while, just happy to finally stop traveling. We can relax here.

And then King's phone buzzes. He glances down.

And his face changes.

I know instantly from his expression that something is wrong.

So deadly wrong.

"He's texted me," King whispers to no one in particular.

We all stop and turn to him.

"Who?" Duke asks his brother.

"*Him.*"

We all know who he means.

GETTING *Duke's phone number was easy for me. Piece of fucking cake.*

All I had to do is send them one simple message to make them fall into my trap. These rich boys think they're so strong. So tough. Who'd ever know someone as little as me can topple the house of Heath-Harding so goddamn easily? With just a few dramatic messages?

Seeing them scramble from their luxury apartment with their little trophy girlfriends was so satisfying to see.

God, I hate them. I hate them all.

And soon they will experience my full hatred.

Soon.

So very soon.

39

DUKE

"Kɪɴɢ, ʀᴇᴀᴅ ᴛʜᴇ ᴍᴇssᴀɢᴇ ᴏᴜᴛ ʟᴏᴜᴅ."

My brother nods and looks back down at his phone. His face betrays how serious the message is. I brace myself for bad news.

This killer is really starting to piss me off.

Next to me, Grace bites her lip nervously. I hate how we're having to do this here, in our family's estate. A place where we should be feeling safe. I hate seeing my girl's face like this, anxious.

"He says he's going to kidnap someone close to me," King reads from his phone. "He says he's someone who's a fan of my work and therefore he's going to target a fan. He's going to do this unless we give the man one million pounds."

I scoff. "A million?"

"This sounds so wrong," Grace says. "A million pounds? This guy isn't interested in money. He's playing with us."

"He's asking for money, though," I reply. "Why else would he be doing that?"

"Simply to play with us. He'll do whatever he wants with or without the money," Grace replies calmly. "Financial gain is secondary to him. The real reward for him is to be seen and to embarrass you."

"Well, he's not making me embarrassed, he's making me fucking angry."

Grace rubs my arm to comfort me.

"We need to talk to the police about this," my brother says. "We'll have to go back to London. Talk to them in person. We have to do it *now*."

"I'll come back with you," I say, already turning for the door.

"And what about us?" Grace asks me. I stop in my tracks. "Are we coming back with you guys?"

Scarlett nods along with her flatmate, agreeing.

We're wasting time arguing. We need to sort this out, and fast.

"It's too dangerous for you two to come back to London," King says. "We're not putting you two in any unnecessary danger."

I nod along with my brother. "I confer."

I can't have them fall into whatever game this killer is playing. I would never forgive myself if something were to happen to my woman.

The girls clearly disagree.

"And you two *aren't* going into danger?" Grace asks, her arms folded defensively.

"If you guys are going back, then we're coming," Scarlett says.

There's no pleasing these two. Can't they see we want to keep them safe?

"You can't keep us here."

"You absolutely can't."

I take Grace's hand and pull her close.

"You're the most important thing in the world for me, Grace," I whisper. "I wouldn't be able to live with myself if something were to happen to you. You need to be safe. You need to stay here."

"But..."

She starts, but I turn to Camilla. We have no time to stay and bicker. King and I need to leave now.

"Please look after them," I plead with my former nanny.

"I will."

The girls are going to say something. They're going to object, but both King and I leave before they do. Us brothers can read the other's mind. We get out before the girls can respond. We turn our backs and immediately walk out of there. The girls are too stunned to follow.

I don't want to do it. I don't want to leave my girl there. I don't want to walk away from her.

I promised Grace that we would be equals.

But her safety is paramount. I can't jeopardize her. I honestly wouldn't be able to live with myself if she got hurt.

"What car shall we go back in?" King asks. "My Aston Martin?"

"How about Father's car?" I suggest. "We can get back to London fast in that thing."

His Lamborghini. He would hate us driving it, but fuck him.

We get in. King drives.

"I feel bad about leaving Grace and Scarlett behind," my brother says as our family's estate disappears from view behind us.

"Me too," I reply. "They may be upset now, but it's better that they're safe with Camilla. She'll look after them."

I feel guilt already eating away at me inside. I just know Grace is going to be pissed.

"Yeah. I just hope they don't do something stupid and put themselves in danger."

"Me too," I say. "Me too."

40

GRACE

I AM SEETHING with unbridled anger.

"How dare the boys drive away like that," I murmur as my hands curl into fists. The sounds of their car fade into the distance beyond the manor, and I am nearly in hysterics. Scarlett is in full agreement with me. She shakes her head.

"I'm going to kill King," she says in a low growl. Oh, she's definitely as angry as me.

They left us. They really fucking left us.

"And I'm going to kill Duke," I reply. "I can't believe it. They promised us they wouldn't do this. They told us they would include us in their plans, but they lied. They *freaking* lied. I really am going to kill him."

I can't believe it. After the promise Duke had made to me. He's really gone and done me dirty.

"We can do their job for them, though," Scarlett suggests. "We don't have to stay stuck here and moping around in this big old place. The boys might've gone to

London, but we can figure out who the killer is after from here."

"Okay, okay. Good." I need something to get my mind off Duke. I sit down at the Heath-Harding dining table and beckon my best friend to join me. "Let's focus on that then instead of our incredibly stupid boyfriends."

"I'll leave you two alone," Camilla says. To be honest, I've completely forgotten she's here in the same room. The woman is a master at blending into the background. I guess that comes after years of practice in the Heath-Harding household. "I feel bad that they left the way they did."

"It's not your fault the boys ran away," I tell her.

She nods and leaves as quietly as she stood in the room.

I don't know how much she agrees with King or Duke or whether she feels as equally angry as Scarlett and me at their sudden disappearance. She really keeps her emotions to herself.

But it's no time to think about that now. Scarlett sits down next to me and pulls out a notepad and pen. "Let's go through that message again and discover who it's about."

I am really going to kill Duke the next time I see him.

* * *

AFTER A LONG TIME of thinking and writing down ideas, we deduce that the killer must be after Giles. Scarlett's former boss at the theater.

Scarlett circles his name on the paper. "He's a fan of King, and the killer did say he's after someone like himself. A fan."

I think about it for a moment. She's right. The killer said he's after a fan of King's. He said he's going after someone close to King, and Giles was always trying to get *close* to the actor. It makes sense. All signs point to him being the victim. I can't see anyone else who fits the same bill as him.

"You know what this means, don't you?" I ask Scarlett.

"Yep."

"You know where we have to go, right? Back to the city. Back to London."

"I think we have no other choice."

"And what are you two planning?"

That was someone else's voice.

Camilla has entered the room, gliding in her special way. Her sudden question makes me jump.

"I think we've discovered who the killer is going after next," I tell her, taking in a deep breath. Camilla's face is unreadable.

"We'll need to go back to London to warn him in time," Scarlett adds.

Camilla's cold expression does not betray what she's thinking. She's standing at the doorway leading out the room. She was told by Duke not to let us leave. To keep us safe. And now she's blocking our only exit out of here.

I don't want to fight her to get out.

"I have never disobeyed an order from a member of the Heath-Harding family in my entire life," Camilla says. My heart drops. I know now that we're going to have to force ourselves out of the manor. But then Camilla continues. "But those boys have made a mistake treating you two like precious dolls. They need you girls. They need you more than they know. I can only say this because I raised them... *fuck the Heath-Harding boys*. I did not raise them to treat their women like this. You have my complete permission to go and get the murdering twat and to show those boys what they've done so very wrong."

To hear her say that makes me want to launch up from my seat and applaud.

"Thank you, Camilla."

"Go, you two. Get the hell out of here."

Scarlett and I both give Camilla a big hug and head past her outside to the manor's garage.

"What car will we use?" Scarlett asks, turning to me.

There's a whole range of vehicles in the Heath-Harding garage. The family has collected some amazing treasures over the years. The best British cars of the last fifty years are on full display in this mini hangar.

But, despite the range of offers available, my eyes fall on one particular car. My eyes light up as I spin back to Scarlett.

"King's Aston Martin," I say. "How about it? He's left it."

"No freaking way, Grace."

"Think about it, Scarlett. His most prized possession. He ran off, leaving us here. So, let's get a little payback."

"Oh, Grace."

The car door's open, but there's no key to the vehicle. King must've taken it back to London with him.

But that's no problem. I've hot-wired a car before, and that's exactly what I do now.

Oh, this is fun. A little bit of payback.

The engine roars to life in my hands. Job done.

"How the hell have you done that?" Scarlett asks me, mouth open in bewilderment.

"It's not the first time I've broken into a car before, Scarlett."

"No way."

"My mum taught me this. She taught me a lot of things."

"You're such a *bad bitch*. I love it."

I flash her a grin and tap the hood of the car. "Now, let's get in, and let's get back to London."

41

GRACE

"Do you know the way to Giles' house?" I ask Scarlett as she drives into London. It's strange to have just been in the city only hours ago and now we're back on the same day. Somewhere amongst this crowd of buildings are our boyfriends. They're probably at a police station right now giving details about the threat. They don't know we're back.

And I don't give a flying fuck. Screw Duke trying to force me to stay locked away. I'm not that kind of girl, and neither is Scarlett.

"I do know where he lives," my best friend replies, turning the steering wheel down a dark street. She pulls out her phone from her handbag. "He sent me the address in an email when I started the job."

"Bit strange for him to do that," I reply.

"Giles is an... odd character, to put it bluntly. I'm not surprised he sent me his address."

"Right."

I take her phone off her and read out the directions.

He's in North London. Quite near Hampstead Heath, actually.

"His place is close to Duke's," I remark. "Near the park."

"Easy to get to," Scarlett says.

"I wonder how we are going to do this. How are we going to tell Giles that we think a killer has him next on his to-be-killed list?"

"I guess we'll show him our evidence for it," Scarlett replies. "Tell him about the text. He's got to believe us."

"We'll have to do this delicately, otherwise we'll look crazy."

"I think we've long gone past the point of crazy, Grace."

"You're telling me."

We drive silently past his address. All the windows of his house are dark. It seems like no one is home. Or the killer has got to him first.

I don't want to think about that.

We park the car a few streets away from his house. It's dark by the time we get out. Night.

"Do you think the killer has already made it here?" I ask Scarlett as we slowly approach Giles' house on foot.

"There's only one way to make sure."

We head up to the front door. It really feels like no one is home.

But then we see the door. It's been left ajar just slightly. No one ever leaves their doors open in London. Ever.

"This is strange," I whisper when we notice the door ajar. "This is wrong."

Inside the house, there is nothing but darkness.

I've really got a bad feeling about this.

Scarlett motions for me to get away from the front door. I follow her to crouch by a hedge outside Giles' house, away from view.

"What do you think has happened?" she asks me, nodding towards the door.

"I honestly don't know, but something definitely feels up. Wrong."

"Well, we can't just knock on that door now and expect everything's fine. What the hell do we do? I don't want to leave here now without making sure the guy's okay, especially when his door's open like that."

I raise my head above the hedge to have another glimpse at Giles' place.

"You sure this is his address?" I ask. "This is definitely Giles' house?"

"Positive," Scarlett replies.

"Okay. Well, I think I see a way inside," I say. "But I don't know if you're going to like it."

I nod towards the side of the house, in the direction of an open window at ground level.

"Oh," Scarlett mutters.

"We could sneak in there," I say. "Snoop around. Make sure he's alright."

"Okay," my best friend replies. "How about I knock on the front door first? If no one answers, then we're squeezing in through the window. I just don't want to feel like a criminal. I don't want to break into the poor guy's place. But I do want to make sure he's alright."

"Sounds good. You wanna knock, or shall I?"

"We're not going to have a *rock, paper, scissors* fight over it," Scarlett whispers. "I'll just do it."

I watch her as she cautiously approaches the open front door, knocks, and then waits for a moment.

I hold my breath. Terrified.

No one answers.

Scarlett comes scrambling back to me.

"Okay," she says. "Window it is."

* * *

THE SPACE between the window is smaller than I thought, but we make it through.

The inside of the house is just what I expect. Dark. Ominous.

We make our way slowly through the place, always on the lookout for Giles. Everything in my body is telling me that there is indeed something very wrong in here. The door. The window. The dark, empty place. Something is certainly not right.

We might be in danger already and don't even know it.

Scarlett and I only communicate through expressions and hand signals as we scour the hallway. We know each other so well. How we move. How we think. All I need is one expression from Scarlett, and I know *exactly* what's on her mind.

It's a slightly strange house. Giles clearly lives on his own. He must've inherited the house or something because it feels old. There's not much stuff here. No real evidence of anything personal for the guy. Not much furniture. The only things that stand out are the stacks of programmes of old theater shows from years past. There's a lot of those filling the hallway, like he's some hoarder or something.

The man definitely likes his theater, that's for sure.

There's a door at the end of the hallway. Some light is escaping from it. It's the only light in the house.

Scarlett turns to me and gestures towards it.

Yep, I'm thinking the same thing.

We approach, and we see that the doorway leads downstairs to the basement.

Jesus.

There's a light on down there.

Here goes.

With a nod, Scarlett lets me lead. I descend one stair at a time, being so damn careful. I don't know what awaits us down here.

I reach the bottom of the staircase, and what greets me makes me gasp.

It's a completely white room. White walls. White ceiling. Like a strange film studio. Close to the staircase is a big camera tripod set up. It's pointing to the middle of the room.

And right there is a chair. And tied to the chair is a woman.

It takes Scarlett whispering her name next to me in shock that I realize who it is bound and gagged there in the center of the white room.

"Penelope?"

The actress who fancied King. The love rival for Scarlett. She's currently tied in a chair right in front of us.

Scarlett and I immediately rush forward to help her. We remove the gag from her mouth. The actress looks dazed, but there are no visible wounds on her. Good.

"You okay?" I ask her.

No response.

Scarlett repeats her name.

"Penelope?"

She just looks a bit dopey. Maybe she's on drugs. She's doesn't look hurt at all.

She whispers something. I notice her lips are dry. We can't make out her words; they're too soft.

Scarlett leans her head in closer.

"What is it, Penelope?"

"He's... still... here..."

"What does she mean?" I ask my best friend. She just looks at me, concerned and completely confused. "Why is she here?"

"I might ask you two the same thing."

Scarlett and I spin around to the voice.

Oh. I get what Penelope was saying. He's still here.

It's Giles. He's standing at the bottom of the stairs.

And that's when I realize he isn't the victim.

He's the killer.

42

GRACE

"Giles..."

Scarlett and I say his name at exactly the same time.

We're trying to talk to the man. Reason with him. Try to understand what's going on and why he might have Penelope Jellis tied up in his basement.

But the theater manager doesn't even let us talk. He doesn't give us the chance to.

Instead, he lets out a guttural roar. Something demonic.

And then he launches into a sprint. Directly towards us.

Fuck.

We barely have time to react. I see an empty chair on the side of the room. I quickly snatch it and throw it awkwardly at the charging man. Giles skids as the chair slams into his legs. He falls.

Neither Scarlett nor I wait to watch him recover. We both grab Penelope's arms and pull the drugged woman to her feet, taking her with us as we pass by Giles struggling to get up on the ground and up the stairs back into the main hallway of his house. Penelope tries to keep up with us on her spaghetti legs.

We hear Giles scraping up off the floor, already recovering from the thrown chair. He's coming to get us.

Holy shit, he's really intending to kill us.

His footsteps echo up the stairs as we flee through his house, trying to escape.

Penelope squeals in terror as we pull her through the hallway.

We make it around the corner and dart into a dark room as Scarlett tries her best to hush her.

"Please be quiet, Penelope. Please."

The actress covers her mouth. She continues to sob loudly, though.

I turn to whisper in Scarlett's ear. "We need to get back to that open window that leads outside," I say. "Where was it?"

My best friend shakes her head. "That window is on the other side of the house."

"Bloody hell."

Behind us, Giles is getting closer. We can hear his feet creak on the old wooden floorboards as he marches through the hallway. He is searching the house for us.

I don't know if he has a weapon. I bet he can overpower us even if he doesn't. He's wiry, but I can see he's strong. There's no way in hell I'm going to risk a physical confrontation with the bloke.

We might be fucking trapped here.

"We need to escape," I whisper urgently. "Right now. We need to get out of this house."

"Follow me," Scarlett says steely.

Both Penelope and I nod and sprint behind her into the next room. We stay silent now, but that means we move slower in order not to make any loud footsteps. We don't dare make a sound alerting the stomping Giles to our whereabouts.

And his stomping is so *loud*. He's so damn close. He doesn't give a fuck that we can hear him.

He means to terrify us.

And it's bloody working.

I hold my breath.

Footstep. Footstep. Footstep.

He's getting closer.

Oh, God. He's so bloody close.

We might not make it out of here.

Daring, we rush down the hallway towards a room. Scarlett opens the door and ushers us through.

Giles's footsteps get even closer. I think he's around the corner. If he turns, then he'll see us all.

"Get out," Scarlett says to us next to the window. "Get help."

"What about you?" I ask her.

"I'll keep him back," my best friend replies.

"What?"

But before I can stop her, Scarlett shuts the door to the room and locks it from the outside. Sealing Penelope and me in. Away from her. Away from Giles.

"Scarlett," I try to whisper through the door. "Scarlett..."

But it's too late. She's gone.

Fuck.

I can't hear anything. I can't hear her footsteps or Giles'.

I've left my best friend alone.

"We need to get out," Penelope says next to me, looking at the open window to our left.

I can't spend time thinking about Scarlett. We're still in danger.

I lead Penelope by the hand to the window. She's still dazed from whatever drugs Giles has plied her with.

I help her with all my strength to climb through the window and into the night's air. Into safety.

"Come out," Penelope pleads as she lies on the grass, her head poking back inside the window. "Come with me."

I stand in the dark room and stare back up at her outside. I shake my head in response. I don't think I can leave. I can't leave my best friend behind to face Giles alone.

I will never leave her.

And then I hear Scarlett scream. Somewhere from deep within the house behind me.

My whole body freezes. It only makes me more determined on my next course of action.

"I'm going back in," I say to Penelope, resolved.

"Leave her," the actress tells me, hissing in the dark. "Come with me instead."

"Go and get help."

"Leave her. She's a goner."

I look at the woman deep in the eyes. She doesn't understand the meaning of friendship. She would never understand why I would never leave my best friend to die alone.

I know what I have to do.

"No. Get help, Penelope."

And with that, I turn and head back to the hallway. Toward the direction of Scarlett's scream.

I find another door. I head through and back into the main hallway. There's no sign of either Scarlett or Giles at all. The scream came from upstairs, and that's where I go.

But I don't even make it up the first stair when I feel the sudden pull of someone grabbing me from behind. A hand covers my mouth. There's a napkin there. I don't even get the chance to scream. I breathe in a smell I've never experienced before.

Fucking hell. Must be chloroform.

That's my last thought, and then my whole world goes dark.

43

DUKE

We've handed in all our evidence to the police in central London and are now back in Father's car heading out of the city. Back to our family manor.

Back to our girls.

"We will need to apologize to our girlfriends," I say to King. He nods sternly, agreeing with my statement. "We really did a wrong thing going to London without them."

"I know. I'm starting to regret that, too."

There was a pit building in my stomach the moment we left the girls behind in the manor to go to London. Guilt. I knew what we had done was wrong the minute we had left the house.

We had promised them both we'll treat them as equals.

And we hadn't done that.

And now we were feeling shit about it. There was only one thing left to do.

Apologize. Grovel. Hope to God they take us back.

"We should have just brought them along," I continue.

"I don't know what the fuck we were thinking... that we could do this ourselves?"

"Us Heath-Harding boys never learn, do we?" King replies with a roll of his eyes.

"Nope," I say. "And I bet those girls are going to give us hell when we get back."

King laughs. "*Hell hath no fury like a woman scorned.*"

I raise an eyebrow at my brother. "Someone knows their Shakespeare. I'm impressed."

"I *am* an actor, remember?"

We chuckle as we join the motorway out of London. It shouldn't be long before we're reunited with the girls. And then we'll really have to brace ourselves for their barbs.

They're really going to be two women very scorned.

King's phone rings. He glances at it, a frown forming.

"Who is it?" I ask.

"Penelope."

"What? The actress in your play? What does she want with you now?"

"Honestly, no clue."

My brother flicks the phone onto loudspeaker and answers. Penelope's rich, defined voice fills the car. In panic.

"He's got them... he's got them."

She's speaking fast. Frantic. Not the measured, posh articulate girl I remember from the theater.

"Slow down, Penelope. What's wrong?" King asks. "Who's got who?"

And then Penelope utters a line that destroys my entire world.

"The killer. Giles. He's got them. He's got the two girls. Scarlett and Grace."

44

GRACE

I WAKE up with a searing pain on my arm. It's uncomfortable. Burning.

As I open my eyes, I try to lift my hands away from the pain, but I can't. They're tied down. I gulp. That's where the pain is coming from.

My wrists are tied.

And I'm sitting in a chair. Restrained to it.

I blink twice, my eyes adjusting to the harsh light blaring into me.

Where am I?

Oh. Now I see.

It takes me a moment to realize I'm in that white room in Giles' basement where we found Penelope. I'm tied to the same chair she was before we rescued her.

I look around me frantically. There's another chair next to me. Probably the same one I threw at Giles. In it sits Scarlett, also restrained by rope like me.

"Scarlett," I whisper. Her eyes are closed. "*Scarlett.*"

She groans and wakes up slowly. She looks a mess. Her hair is everywhere, and her makeup is smeared across her face. I guess I probably look the same.

Someone coughs.

I glance up. At them.

And that's when I see the barrel of the gun pointing directly at my face. A chrome-black pistol.

"Wakey wakey, Grace."

It's Giles aiming the gun at me from a few feet away. He has a nasty smile plastered over his ugly face.

"Giles?"

"Yep. It's me. Hello dear. Had a nice beauty sleep?"

"Let us go," Scarlett whispers. Her voice is raspy. We've both been through hell.

And we're definitely not out of it yet.

Giles tuts. He keeps the gun level at my face. I wish I can swipe out at him with my arm and take him off his feet. I wish I can force that gun out of his hands, but I am so securely fastened to this chair that I can't do shit. I struggle against my restraints, to no avail.

Feck.

"I didn't expect both of you to come," Giles says. "And so bloody soon as well. You two are smart deciphering that threat I sent to your handsome boyfriend, Scarlett. Such a shame those boys aren't as smart as either of you. But, in the end, you two made things so easy for me walking right into here as you did. You might be smarter than your boyfriends, but you're both stupid. I have you both now. You did give me a little fright when you came down here, I have to admit, but there's nothing a little chloroform can't fix."

Yep, that must've been what that weird substance was on that tissue he stuffed my mouth with as I climbed the stairs earlier after Scarlett. I'd guessed right.

"You drugged us?" I ask the man.

"Oh, I had to," Giles replies. He's loving talking to us like dumb children. He wants to show off his little success. "Dear Scarlett over here was screaming her head off and you were so determined to find her. Naturally, I had to stop you both somehow. I know it's such an uncivilized way, but *desperate times*, you know."

"You're the one who killed Ben," Scarlett mutters. "You're the one who's been stalking us this entire time. You're the asshole who's been sending us those horrible threats."

Giles grins. "Bingo! Of course I did! Oh, that was so much fun. A tiny bit of drama. Did it work? Were you guys afraid? Confused? I hope you were. That was the plan."

"Why are you doing this?" I ask him. "Why are you causing all this pain and misery? What do you gain from it?"

Giles looks at me and sighs loudly, like I'm stupid.

"I've been watching the Heath-Harding boys so carefully for ages now, even before you two came along. Watching intensely. Those two boys getting everything they've ever wanted in life has really rattled my bones, and then them finding love on top of it all. It's just so... *unfair*. Good looking and rich and talented? Come on. What about the little guys like me who have to beg for scraps? Guys like me who haven't been shagged in years? Those Heath-Harding boys are so incredibly greedy, I just had to do something about it. And that's why I've carried out my plans. Unlike you two and those boys, I am smart. I may not have the looks or money or family name like the Heath-Hardings, but I do know how to pull off the crime of the century."

I struggle against the restraints again. They don't budge.

"You're crazy," I say. "Let us go. We've done nothing to you."

Giles doesn't pay any heed to my protests and continues his insane monologue.

"I am going to make both Duke and King feel the pain they deserve. It was very bad of you two to get Penelope out of this house just then. That has royally screwed up my plans. I'll let you know. I *was* hoping to make a film of her as a little actress playing out a script I'd written for her. That would've been fun. She ignored me at the theater, but for a brief moment she was all mine to do whatever I wanted with her. Well, that was until you two came along."

"What do you want with us?" Scarlett asks.

Giles ignores her as well and carries on with his spiel. It's like he's been keeping all these thoughts inside himself and now they're bursting like a dam. And Scarlett and I are his unwilling audience.

"Penelope was especially easy to kidnap the other day," Giles continues. "It's a shame she's gone now, but it doesn't matter that I've lost her when I've gained you girls. You two are an even better prize than some squealing actress harlot. I've actually scored the girlfriends of the boys I hate most in the world. How fantastic is that? I'm going to enjoy watching each of them die. I can't do it here though, it's compromised. I will have to take you somewhere to kill you. I'll take you two to the Heath."

Hampstead Heath?

BUZZ!

My phone rings in my pocket.

All of us freeze. Scarlett looks at me, horrified. Giles lowers his gun.

Without the courtesy of asking me, the man reaches over and pulls the phone from my pocket. He waves the device in front of my face. I see the name on my screen.

I turn to Scarlett.

"It's Duke."

Giles laughs. "Don't get your hopes up, miss Grace. I bet the brothers have spoken to Penelope already. I bet they're heading here right now, but they're too late. So how about we have a bit of fun, shall we? I want you to talk to your little boyfriend. I want him to hear your voice and suffer."

To emphasize his point, he presses the nozzle of the gun up against my forehead. I flinch back.

"Answer it," Giles says. "But don't say shit, you understand?"

I nod. I'll agree to anything to hear Duke.

Giles presses the loudspeaker button.

"Grace, Grace. You okay?"

Hearing Duke's voice - even with a gun against my head - makes me feel safer. He can calm me in even the worst of situations.

"I'm tied up, Duke."

"Are you hurt? Where are you?"

"Hello, mister Heath-Harding," Giles interrupts.

"Giles?" That's King's voice. Scarlett straightens up in her seat. "I swear to God if you lay one finger on them."

"You will do *nothing*," Giles mocks. "You can't do shit. I'm in control now, even with all your money and power. You all have to listen to me now. I'm the one who's boss now."

"Have you hurt them?" King asks. "Are they okay?"

"Your girls are perfectly fine... still. But how long will that be? I don't know."

"What do you want, Giles?" That's Duke again. His voice is stern and business-like. No emotion. He's gone into action mode. "What can we offer you?"

"Oh, I want you to know how much your precious girls are going to suffer. I want to listen to you talk to them for the very last time. Say your goodbyes, because there won't be another chance."

"Grace..."

I leap into action. It's not just Duke that can do that.

"Duke, if there is anything I could do right now, it would be to watch you play catch with Jack and Anna. You remember when I watched you do that?"

"I do."

"You remember where?"

"Yes. That was a good day."

"It was," I reply. "That's where I wish I could go to right now." Tears come streaming down my face as I talk towards the phone. He seems so far away. So distant. I wish I could hold him one last time. "Duke, I love you."

"I..."

Giles hangs up before Duke can finish his sentence. I know that the situation is crazy - that the wanker's literally got a gun focused on my head - but him cutting short Duke telling me he loves me pisses me off most of all.

"Enough. That's disgusting enough," Giles mutters.

"You could've let me say goodbye to King," Scarlett angrily says to the man.

"Not enough time. You two have had enough fun already," Giles sneers back. "I think your boyfriends have heard plenty. Don't say I'm not a generous man. Alright, let's go and kill you both, shall we?"

45

GRACE

Giles is true to his word. He takes us to Hampstead Heath. It's just around the corner from his house. From Duke's house. I still can't believe they live so close to each other. The man behind all those threats has been practically neighbors to us all this time and we never even suspected a thing.

It's night, so there's little chance of bumping into someone or a neighbor seeing us. If they did look out their window, they would've only seen Giles walking close behind Scarlett and me. They wouldn't see the gun in his pocket aimed at our backs. They wouldn't hear his hushed threats whispered into our ears.

Scarlett reaches over to hold my hand as we get to the park's gate.

"Don't touch each other," Giles warns. "Go inside the park. Stay apart."

"Okay," Scarlett whispers back. She looks at me, concerned. I wish we could properly talk to each other. I wish we could plan something. But Giles is keeping a close eye on us.

Let's go and kill you both.

That's what he told us. It's like I'm walking in a dream. Nothing feels real. There's a gun pointed at my back and I can't even begin to process it.

I'm going to die. I'm going to die. I'm going to die.

"Don't even try to escape," Giles sneers from behind us. "Even if one of you makes it far, I'll just drop the other with a single shot. *Bang.*"

Scarlett dares to turn around and face him as we take a step into the park.

"Penelope has escaped already," she says. "Even if you kill us both, you are still doomed. The boys are on their way, and so is the police, I imagine."

Giles tilts his head back and laughs. "I rather prefer to be infamous for killing the girls of the Heath-Harding boys than anything else," he says. "That'll secure my name in history. My name will be forever linked with such a noble family. They won't be able to escape that."

"Well, if you're going to kill us," I say. "Then can I make one simple last request?"

"What do you mean?"

"A sort of final meal, but as a request of where to take us to shoot us?"

"Oh, I like this," Giles replies with a grin. "Where is it? Far?"

"Not far at all." I gesture to the left of us, deeper in the park. "Kill us on top of Parliament Hill."

He narrows his eyes. He's suspicious. "Why there?"

"Call me sentimental, but I'll like to die looking at a view of London," I reply. I keep a stony expression etched on my face.

Please say yes.

Giles frowns, thinking for a moment.

"Alright. That will be a very dramatic place for your silly boyfriends to find your lifeless bodies, I must say. Up Parliament Hill we go. Quickly now, and remember to stay apart."

As we turn towards the landmark, Scarlett quickly whispers to me.

"I hope you know what you're doing."

I wink back confidently, but I certainly don't feel it on the inside.

My God, I really hope this works.

We head up the Hill, all the time knowing that there's a handgun pointed at our backs. We get to the very top, where there are benches overlooking the city.

Unlike daytime, when there's usually lots of tourists that flock to this famous view, now there are no other people around. We're alone.

Alone to die.

Well, at least it's a beautiful place to go. The city lights twinkle in the distance. What an amazing place to have lived.

Well, if this is it, then at least I've lived a good life.

"At least I'm dying with my best friend beside me," I whisper to Scarlett.

We're both crying.

"I'll see you on the other side," she whispers back.

We don't care about Giles' warning about touching anymore. What the fuck can he do about it now? We grab each other's hand.

He doesn't care about our contact; Giles is rambling now. He's excited. Running on the fumes of his plan's victory. Giddy at the thought of shooting us both.

"My name will be next to Heath-Harding in the history books now. All the papers tomorrow will have me as a headline. I'll be famous, no matter what King and Duke might try. They won't be able to scrub me out of their little family history. Nothing their money or their power or influence can do to stop me from forever being linked with them. You know, there might even be a Netflix documentary made about me. You two will just be grainy photos that they'll use. My face will be everywhere. A boogeyman to frighten children. Ha!"

I ignore the mad man and just look into Scarlett's eyes one last time. Taking her in. I hold her hand tight. She smiles weakly at me, putting on a brave face. I do the same.

"Goodbye, Scarlett."

"Goodbye, Grace."

Giles marches up to us, forcing us apart with a push of his hand. He waves his gun around theatrically.

"Alright, let's do King's girl first, shall we?"

"No," I yell.

I want to be first. I want to give Scarlett a chance to escape.

But Giles is already raising his gun. He aims it at Scarlett.

Not her first.

He smiles as he fires the gun.

And I dive forward.

Between the gun and my best friend.

I get hit by the bullet. I feel the force of something heavy push into my body. It's like being shot with a hundred footballs.

I fall to the ground. Intense pain courses from my shoulder to the rest of my body. Pain I have never experienced before.

Is this how painful dying is?

Giles is standing in front of me. Open-mouthed at my body.

I can't see Scarlett.

Where is she? Did she run? Is she safe?

Everything starts to spin. My vision goes all blurry.

Ah. I really must be dying.

And that's when I see the two shadows burst out of the bushes.

The last image I see before everything goes dark is of two tall muscular frames darting out of the darkness to cover Giles. They tackle him to the ground.

King?

Duke?

And then blackness.

46

GRACE

THE FIRST THING I hear is beeping. Loud, continuous beeping.

And I want it to stop.

My head feels full. It's like I don't know who I am or where I am. Everything hurts.

Ouch.

Where the hell am I? Why can't I feel or see or hear anything except this bloody noise?

And then I wake up properly. It's like I'm coming up for air after a long swim underwater. It all takes me a moment to remember the details of what's happened to me.

Hampstead Heath.

Parliament Hill.

Giles.

The gun.

The shot.

The pain.

Damn. All of that. Does that mean I'm dead right now?

Awoken, I blink open my eyes and unwelcome light greets me.

Hang on. I'm still alive? How can that be?

The first person I see is Scarlett sitting opposite me on my bed.

I'm lying on a bed? A soft bed?

Scarlett?

She's smiling at me. A grin that stretches from ear to ear.

"Grace? You okay?"

I try to speak, but all that comes out of my mouth is a long groan.

"Guys," Scarlett yells out a doorway behind her. "Guys, she's awake. She's trying to talk."

Guys? Who? What's going on?

My eyes dart from my best friend calling out the door and I take the moment to survey my surroundings. I'm in a small room. The beeping noise that so bloody annoys me is coming from machines around my bed.

"I'm... in... hospital?"

I manage to speak. Slowly. Painfully.

Everything hurts like hell.

My best friend turns back to me and nods.

"You're in hospital, Grace. You're alive. You're going to be okay. It was a bit scary there for a moment - well, for a bit more than a moment - but you're going to be okay now."

She reaches out and takes my hand. I try to squeeze my fingers around hers, but I can't. It's so much effort and it feels like I've got no energy left in my body. I feel so empty. Hollow. Not like me at all.

That bullet from Giles' gun must've really taken me out.

Behind Scarlett, the door bangs open and in rushes King.

And Duke.

There he is. I thought I would never see that handsome face again.

Concern is deeply etched on their faces. Duke sprints to my side, his eyes traveling me up and down. I try to smile when I see him.

His handsome face is the best thing I've seen in a very long time.

"You alright, Grace?" he asks me. "Are you okay?"

I've never seen the man so panicked and frantic. He's acting so out of character. He's no longer cool and collected and confident.

He's *scared*. For me. He wants to protect me. He wants to make sure I'm okay.

I just nod in reply. Words are too hard to form right now.

And Duke breathes a long sigh of relief. It's like he's finally breathing again after days of holding air in his lungs.

"I understood your message on the phone, Grace," Duke says. His hand finds my shoulder. "When you told me about playing with Damien's kids on the top of Parliament Hill. I knew you'd somehow be up there. I *know* you, Grace."

"Both King and Duke tackled Giles to the ground when he shot you," Scarlett exclaims, eager to tell the story. "They arrived just in time. Giles never got the chance to let off another shot."

"We heard the gunshot and immediately knew where you were," King says. "We were already heading in that direction, thanks to you and your coded message."

"You dived to save my life, Grace." Scarlett's got tears in her eyes. "Thank you."

"You were lucky," Duke continues. "Giles was aiming right at Scarlett's heart. He couldn't miss at that distance, but because you dived in front of the gun, then it only hit your shoulder. It was still a bad place to get shot at, but much better than Scarlett's heart, I reckon."

"Get it?" Scarlett asks. "Scarlett's heart? Scarlett Hart?"

I shake my head and moan again. "Not... funny."

"Good to see your humor returning," King remarks.

I try to speak. "And... Giles?"

"Don't worry, we got him," Duke whispers to me. Relief floods through me. "We nailed the bastard. He's in police custody now. Penelope is a witness. We've got our best lawyers on it. There's enough evidence to make sure he's going to go away for a very long time. You will never see that twat ever again."

"There might be a Netflix documentary about him," Scarlett says. "But it will only be about how pathetic he is."

"Good."

But I no longer care about that guy. I'm just happy to see everyone that I love safe, even if they're desperate to tell me everything that's happened.

Scarlett exhales and holds my hand tighter. "I owe my life to you, Grace."

I see that there are tears in her eyes. I start to well up as well.

"You've been... my best friend," I reply softly. "There's nothing more I want than that."

She smiles. "Me too."

"We better give Grace and Duke a moment together," King suggests, placing his hand on Scarlett's. She nods and lets go of mine.

"I'll only be outside," she tells me. "I'll see you soon when you're better rested."

When they leave the room, Duke edges even closer to my face.

He really is a sight to behold. My savior. My love.

He's here, and that's all I need.

"Grace. I need to say something to you."

"What?"

Duke's face is like stone. He's so serious. "I am sorry."

"For what? You just saved my life."

"I'm sorry for the way that I acted before you were taken. How I got King and me to leave you two alone at the manor. I shouldn't have left you there. I should've included you in our plans. I made a promise, and I broke it. I'm sorry."

I look into his bright blue eyes - the same eyes that made me fall in love with him all those years ago - and I smile.

"That was a nice little speech there," I whisper. "Did you rehearse that in the mirror?"

He shrugs. "Kinda. I wanted to make it special. You know that Scarlett made King practically get on his knees to apologize."

"You'll do that for me, too?"

The man growls.

"I'll do a lot of things to make you happy, Grace. But I get on my knees for no one."

"We'll see about that," I say, before leaning my mouth towards his ear. "Maybe we can try that in the bedroom."

Duke raises an eyebrow. "So, you've forgiven me?"

"Well, you did save my life," I say. "I do forgive you."

"Good. I have a present for you."

"A present?"

Duke stands up and heads towards the door. "A little bit of a loud present, sorry."

He opens the door and calls out into the hallway. I hear the scraping of fast little feet on the hospital floor.

I know who this is...

And then Jack and Anna come swarming into my room. They dart towards my bed, arms outstretched for a big hug.

"Grace!"

"Careful guys, she's pretty delicate," Duke says.

"Nonsense," I reply. "I can handle these two."

The kids squeeze the living daylights out of me, but I love it. My heart is full.

I spot Audrey in the doorway, smiling at Duke.

And I know everything is going to be alright.

* * *

An hour later, after playtime with the kids and they've been pulled off my bed and sent home, it's just Duke and I alone again in my room. I'm exhausted. My body really needs to rest.

Duke doesn't say a thing. He knows how tired I am. He just pulls up a chair and sits next to me, staring at me with his trademark intense stare.

"It's nice to see the kids again," I say.

"Yep."

There's a long pause. We just sit there in comfortable silence together.

"I told King and Camilla about Damien," Duke says eventually. "I told them everything that happened."

"You did?"

"I told them about the boarding school incident and our correspondence. I even told them about his family and what I've been doing for them for the last few years."

I smile weakly. "I'm glad you did, Duke. I'm glad you told them."

"King and Camilla agree that it's best for me to continue looking after them. I guess I never told them because I was once ashamed of what I'd done and how we'd lost Damien. But you've made things clear to me. You've made me see how happy it can be to just make things *right*. I don't need to worry about my reputation or for what I did years ago, thanks to you."

He leans over and tenderly kisses my forehead, and my eyes start to drift close.

I fall asleep to Duke holding my hand.

47

DUKE

FATHER CAME to visit us at the hospital. My father. The man of no emotions for the past twenty years. He actually turned up. Sure, I invited him to come and see Grace, but I never thought he'd turn up. He's never done it in the past.

"How is she?" he asks when he turns up at the hospital.

"She's asleep," I reply, ushering him out of Grace's room. We stand in the corner of the hallway outside. King joins us. Scarlett watches on nervously from the waiting room.

Father is wearing a Savile Row tailored suit from the same people who've done mine. Those expensive suits are an indulgence for the men of the Heath-Harding family. He's a handsome man, even at his age. Clean-shaven. Strong jaw. Peppered hair. A true silver fox. King and I have clearly inherited our looks from him.

"Is she going to be okay?" he asks me quietly.

I nod. Even though he's turned up here in what seems

to be a kind act, I'm still very cautious around him. I don't trust my father. "She's going to be fine, just a little shaken."

"Good. I can always arrange to have her taken to a private hospital. Maybe a specialist one in America if needs be."

"We don't want anything of the sort," I reply. I can already feel my voice rising. Bickering with the man in the middle of the hospital is not idyllic. "Let's go to the pub next door."

King agrees, and so does Father.

WE SIT down in a tucked-away booth in the pub next to the hospital with a fine bottle of Scotch bought from the bar. I've chosen these seats deliberately as we're out of sight and earshot of anyone else in the pub just so that if this conversation turns to an argument, then we're far enough from others to matter.

I pour Father and King a glass before one for myself. We cheer somberly.

"Why are you here, Father?" It's my opening question from him. It's blunt, I know. But our family has never had the time for niceties.

He takes in a deep breath before he answers me. He's not himself today. He's not loud or brash or commanding. He's different. I'm still yet to uncover whether it's genuine or just an act.

"I heard about what happened to your girlfriend."

"Her name is Grace."

"I heard what happened to *Grace*, and I thought I should visit."

"And you decided to turn up to the hospital out of the blue after years avoiding my brother and me to make yourself seem like a caring human being? How *very* noble of you, Father. It's too much for our hearts to bear."

"Feel free to mock me as much as you wish," he says. "I've come on good terms."

"Oh, we will mock you. You've literally distanced your-self for years, Father. What did you think our reaction would be?"

Next to me, King is silent. I know him well enough to understand he's agreeing with every one of my words. He's just patiently waiting to see how Father reacts.

"I think I need to clear up things," Father says.

"You think?"

He coughs. "I'm sorry."

King and I sit in utter silence.

Those truly are the last words I could ever imagine emerging from in between my father's lips.

I'm sorry.

This is a man who's never apologized in his entire life, and here he is in some dingy pub, finally accepting respon-sibility.

It's a rarer sight than seeing the bloody Yeti.

"What?"

"I am sorry, boys."

"Care to elaborate?" King asks.

None of us have properly touched our drinks yet.

Father leans forward. He cups his face with his hands. For a moment, I feel like he's wiping away a tear.

He might actually be crying.

Holy fucking shit.

"Hearing the news," he says, his voice tiny. "Hearing what had nearly happened to you both and your girlfriends made me realize how bloody close I was to losing the only family I have left. It's made me come to realize things.

Certain things that I should've taken notice of a long time ago. It's given me pause to think."

Now I'm curious.

"Think about what?"

"Of how I've behaved since... your mother passed."

"Father, that was decades ago," King says.

Father turns to him and that's when we see how blood-shot the man's eyes are. He's actually been bloody crying.

"I know it's been a long time, but I've always wanted to tell you both that I took your mother's death hard. Very hard."

"Well, it's too late to tell us now," I retort. I can't deal with all this coming from the man. He's now being humble?

"And I am sorry for that as well," Father replies. "I've only come to realize it in the wake of the recent events. I know that's wrong, and I am sorry."

I still don't trust the man. He can brandy around as many pretty words as he likes, but his actions over the years have been proof enough of how little he cares or regards my brother and me. King seems to agree.

"I don't know if we can believe you," King interjects.

"I wouldn't blame you if you couldn't," Father replies. "But I'm being honest here. As honest as I've ever been. I've missed you two. I tried to farm you out when you were boys so that I didn't have to raise you, but the real truth is that I couldn't possibly even *look* at you both."

"No, you couldn't," I say. "That much was clear."

"I couldn't look at you both because you remind me of *her*," Father replies. He's ashen-faced now. A man defeated by time and emotion. He's hunched over his glass. I've never seen the proud man like this before. I've never seen him emotional before. Or weak. Or vulnerable. He's definitely all three now.

"Her?" King asks.

"Your mother. I see so much of her in you both. Always have. When she died, I just couldn't stand looking at you both because you are reflections of her. The woman I love who I couldn't save, not with all the money and power in the world. You two reminded me of my failings as a husband and as a father. I see your mother in you both every time I look into your faces, even now. You two are both kind and good-hearted like her. You have her soul."

King and I sit amazed.

Here's our Father. The man who gives fiery speeches in Parliament. The man who owns half of England. The man whose heart has been sealed off for many years.

And he's apologizing to us? He's telling us his deepest secrets and fears?

He's telling us we remind him of our mother, and that's why he's been like he's been for all these years?

I turn to my brother, and I know there's one question we're both thinking about.

Do we forgive him?

* * *

"THIS MUST BE GRACE."

Father shakes my girl's hand as she sits upright on her hospital bed.

She smiles up at him in that radiant way only she can.

"And you must be Lord Heath-Harding?"

"Please, call me Earl. It's a pleasure to meet you."

Grace's eyes dart to mine. I know what she's thinking.

Please don't make fun of his name as well.

"Lovely to meet you likewise, Earl."

"I've heard and read a lot about you, Grace. How you very nearly sacrificed yourself for your best friend."

"Scarlett would've done the same for me."

"It's a very commendable attribute."

"Thank you."

Father gestures around at all the hospital machinery surrounding Grace.

"I won't take up any more of your time, Grace. I'm sure you want to rest," he says. "But I can promise you we're definitely going to meet again. I'm very much looking forward to having a proper conversation with such an amazing young lady."

Oh, Grace *loves* being called a lady. Her pretty eyes light up.

She understands now where King and I get our gentlemanly manners from.

"Thank you, Earl. Likewise."

I guide Father outside before turning around to close the door to Grace's room. I wink at her, and she happily mouths back *lady* to me.

She's never going to let that go, is she?

"That's a beautiful woman you've got there," Father tells me in the hospital hallway.

"I know."

"You're a lucky man."

"I know."

He pats me on the shoulder and reaches for a handshake. I look down at his invitation.

And then I shake his hand.

We've never done this before.

It's going to take King and me some time to fully come to terms with Father, but now we're on the road to recovering our relationship. Everything looks positive.

Life looks positive.

But there's still one *teeny tiny* thing left to resolve.

Grace.

48

GRACE

I'M NEEDED in hospital for another week. Tests and things. I recover quicker than even the doctors thought possible. Well, it's only because I want to get out there and live the rest of my life. I hate that room. I want to be with Duke. I want to be free.

Duke and Scarlett both refuse to leave my bedside for the past week. King has been delegated - against his will - to be food courier. It's funny seeing the proud actor having to deliver burgers and fries across town.

Duke always talks with the doctors at every chance he can get. The man is insistent that I receive the best care possible. He does not rest until he makes sure I'm okay or that I have everything I need. He's action man. Even though I protest and say I can handle my own needs, *thank you very much*, he completely ignores me and tries to help me in any way he can. And I love him for that.

And then, after one of the longest weeks of my entire life, I'm finally ready to be discharged.

"Good," I say, sitting up in my hospital bed when I receive the news. "It's Wednesday and I have a tour to run tonight. Perfect timing."

Duke shakes his head at me.

"Grace, you need to take things easy. Maybe you should spend another week at home. Get some rest before you head out and start doing your tours again."

I glare at the man. "Excuse me? I'm Grace Madden. I won't dare take a week of *rest*."

"Well, can I at least drive you from the hospital?" Duke asks. "Or are you planning to run a marathon home?"

I roll my eyes and get standing on my feet.

"I can pay for my own taxi home."

"Grace, I'm offering to drive you."

I glower at him. "Okay. Fine."

I step into the hospital hallway where Scarlett and King are waiting for me. They give me a big hug. It's very sweet.

"Thanks for everything you two have done for me the last few weeks," I whisper to them.

They both nod and let me go.

"I'll see you soon," Scarlett tells me.

Duke takes my hand and guides me down the hallway. I try to walk straight and fast like my usual self, but I'm still weak from the bullet. My walk is now slow and awkward. It's annoying for anyone to see this, especially Duke. But the man doesn't show it. He just calmly and quietly walks alongside me at my pace, never uttering a word about my struggle.

God, he is perfect, isn't he?

He leads me to his parked car. We get in. I take a long time to do so on account of my body working much slower than I want it to.

And then we're off and away.

"Um, shouldn't you have taken a right there?" I ask him

as Duke drives us through London's traffic. I swear he's just missed a turning for his road.

"I'm going a different way today," he replies calmly.

Oh. I'm bloody suspicious.

"I'm sure you've missed the turning for your place," I retort. "You're being a pretty crap taxi service, I must say."

Duke turns to me and smiles.

"I've got a surprise for you, Grace."

"Oh no. What is it? I hate surprises, especially the ones where you are all smug about it. Last time this happened, I ended up discovering you're keeping a secret family in the middle of England."

"I'm not saying a word until we reach there."

"Please tell me. Please tell me, Duke."

"Nope."

"*Please.*"

But he doesn't respond to my interrogation.

Not until we arrive outside the gates of an airport.

49

GRACE

There's a private plane waiting for us at the airport.

An actual *freaking* private plane.

"Is that just for us two?" I ask the man as we step out of his car and onto the tarmac of the airport runway. My mouth is hanging open at the sight of the jet sitting there, ready for us.

"Yes. Just for us," Duke replies. His sharp blue eyes are on me, and I shiver with anticipation.

Where is this gorgeous hunk taking me?

"You're taking me on a trip?" I ask.

"What do you think I'm doing, Grace?"

"No bloody way. Where to?"

Duke smiles and offers me his hand. "You'll see. Follow me."

Gosh, I feel like a princess.

We walk up the stairs into the cabin of the private plane. I can't stop swearing and cheering as we head inside. This is so crazy.

I would never have thought, in a million years, that I would get the chance to ride in a private plane.

And now, here I am with the man I love. Blimey.

I giggle as I sit down on the long couch inside, feeling the plush seating in disbelief. On the table in the middle of the cabin is a bottle of champagne in an ice bucket with two glasses ready just for us. I look around the plane as Duke pours us a glass of bubbly. He chats to the pilot for a moment and the plane gets ready to depart.

"I really can't believe this," I exclaim as Duke passes me a glass of champagne. "You've really outdone yourself this time, Duke."

Oh, he certainly knows it. He gives me a sexy wink.

We chink our glasses together and sip.

"I'm going to make your dream holiday a reality," he says to me. "It's the least I can do after what you did on Parliament Hill."

I start to cry. I'm overcome with emotion. "Thank you."

"You know that Scarlett had a hand in all of this," he tells me. "She's practically organized the whole thing herself. She really loves you, Grace."

"I know."

What could this be? Where could he be taking me?

The flight takes off, but I don't even notice. My attention is on other things.

Mainly on Duke's drop-dead gorgeous body.

He's closed the door between the cabin and the cockpit before take-off so that we're given complete privacy. And I very much intend to use the time alone.

I place my champagne glass on the table beside us and I swing one leg over the man so that I'm sitting in his lap facing him.

"Hello, Grace."

"Hello, Duke."

We kiss.

Duke's hands eagerly travel down my back, heading straight for my ass.

Oh, we're going to fuck on a private plane...

I let him slowly remove my dress as our tongues meet. His fingers are delicate and gentle as he removes my clothing until I'm in nothing but my bra and panties. I feel so naked in front of him. It puts me in heat.

I'm so horny.

"Take those off," my man commands me in a low voice.

What else can I do? I obey the hunk.

With his stare never flinching from my body, Duke begins to unbutton his suit in that masculine way of his.

Damn, he's so bloody sexy.

I just can't help myself. My hands fly to his exposed chest to feel his firm muscles. They ripple against my touch.

He's like Superman on steroids.

He unzips his pants, and his erection swings out.

"Lower yourself on me," Duke demands.

Again, I obey.

I shudder and moan loudly as I sit on his cock, and he enters me. I lean back to take him in completely and Duke's hands hold me in place, stopping me from falling.

"We're doing this at a hundred miles an hour," Duke whispers in my ear. "The world is rushing past below our feet."

The thought turns me on even more.

No one knows we're doing this...

"This is some mile high club," I reply.

We're being so damn naughty...

Duke pushes in deep inside me. I steady myself with my hands on his shoulders as he fucks me hard.

"This is just a taste of what life with me is like," the man says.

"This is some taste, big boy."

* * *

WE'RE in the air for a few hours. And then we're landing. Somewhere sunny. Somewhere hot.

It doesn't take long of me looking out the plane window to realize where we are. I recognize the landmarks. The architecture. It's somewhere I've never been, but where I've been dreaming about for years.

"Rome?" I ask Duke. "We're in Rome?"

"Yep."

I am so giddy with excitement that I practically leap out of the plane.

Of course, in typical Duke fashion, there's a limousine waiting for us on the runway.

"Get in," Duke says, nodding at the vehicle.

He doesn't have to tell me twice.

The car speeds down the streets of Rome with us two in the back. Moments earlier we were making love in our own private jet, and next, we're zooming through an ancient European city in the back of a limo.

Things don't get any crazier than this.

It's a real taste of Duke's life.

"You need to tell me where we're going, Duke," I say to the man.

"I can't. It'll ruin the surprise."

We arrive in front of the Vatican.

"What?"

I can't contain myself.

Duke opens my side door and helps me out.

"I've booked the Sistine Chapel, Grace. A private tour, just for us."

"Wait... how have you managed that?"

"Well, the Heath-Harding family and the Catholic Church have some history over the centuries. Let's just say that they owe us a few favors."

"Oh."

"You told both Scarlett and me of how you've always wanted to come because of how your mother came here when she was your age," Duke says.

"She said it was her favorite place in the world. I've been saving to come here for ages," I reply.

"Well," Duke says as he leads me through the doors and down the staircase into the empty Chapel. "Now you're here."

The small room that is the ancient Chapel is truly breathtaking. No wonder it's known as one of the pinnacle masterpieces of human history.

Wow.

Michelangelo truly was an artistic genius.

I look up at his beautiful ceiling in amazement. This is what my mother once had seen. I can see why she loved it here. I feel so close to her, even though she's gone. She once stood in this spot and looked up, just as I'm doing now.

It's so dazzling. So incredible.

"I can't believe I'm standing here," I say. My voice carries around the room.

There's no one else in here except for Duke and me.

And then, below Michelangelo's ceiling in my mother's favorite place in the whole wide world, Duke Heath-Harding gets down on one knee in front of me.

"Will you marry me, Grace Madden?"

And I, naturally, say yes.

EPILOGUE

ONE YEAR LATER

DUKE

I'm waiting for Grace by the cathedral altar, and I am nervous.

I am never nervous, but today is the most important day of my life. Hey, I am allowed to feel a bit anxious on my wedding day.

It doesn't help that we're getting married in St Paul's Cathedral. My family's connection to this place stretches back generations. Usually, it's only royalty that can get married here, but when you're a Heath-Harding, a lot of doors open to you. They *swing* open.

"You're okay, Duke?" King asks me as he stands next to me by the altar. "You look like you're shaking."

I growl at him in response. He's my Best Man, but he's still eager to tease me for any display of nerves. I guess it's tradition now to mess with the Groom. I was Best Man at his wedding a few months ago to Scarlett and - trust me - I did not let him off lightly then.

That was a beautiful wedding. The two had it in Kew Gardens, an amazing park in London. It was a sunny Spring day. Both Scarlett and Grace looked stunning in their dresses. To see their friendship blossom has touched even my cold heart.

The Cathedral today is full of guests. Distant family members. Other aristocratic families. Even my father is in the front row.

Camilla is here as well. I made sure she has one of the best seats in the place. She sits there, smiling at me. She looks so happy to be here. She told me this morning in a whisper that she knows my mum is up there somewhere watching down on this with a twinkle in her eye.

It was the best conversation I've ever had with Camilla. I'm glad she's here. Out of everyone except for Grace and King, she's the one who knows me the most. To have her blessing for our marriage is a gift.

I give her a cheeky wink. She winks back.

There's also a big Cockney guy in the front row. I don't know why Grace has decided to invite the man who owns the fish and chip shop below her flat to her wedding, but I can't argue with her. She just told me he's gotten her out of a lot of dodgy situations in the past and therefore deserves a place on the front row.

I dread to think about what *kind* of situations.

I don't have any time to think of big Cockney guys. The wedding starts, and my nerves begin to grow.

But all anxiety leaves me the moment I see Grace coming down the Cathedral aisle.

Instead of a father escorting her, it's Audrey, Jack, and Anna. The kids are dressed in a tiny suit and dress. They look incredibly cute. This was all Grace's idea, and the kids took to it like duck to water. They love the fact they get to bring her down the aisle to me. Scarlett's here as Maid of Honor. I heard their bachelorette party was pretty wild, but right now, she looks gorgeous. Scarlett is now the manager of the theater. She was promoted up the company. She's now got her dream job in her dream city and she's so incredibly happy.

Everyone's eyes are on Grace. And she is beautiful. Her dress is simple, yet elegant. She's still got that spark in her eyes I've come to love. Like she's ready to bite my hand off if I dare embarrass her.

"This is insane," she whispers to me when she reaches the altar.

I laugh.

"I love you," I reply. "You look beautiful."

Grace blushes. Damn, she looks so adorable.

"We're really doing this," she mutters. "We're really actually *bloody* doing this."

"Welcome to the family," I say. "You're a Heath-Harding now."

* * *

Everything is perfect. The ceremony is perfect. Seeing my friends and family is perfect. Camilla's face is perfect when King does his Best Man's speech and mentions her multiple times. Oh, she doesn't like that kind of attention.

And then we're at the best part of the day. The party.

There's a band playing on stage, and we dance late into the night. Even Grace is on the dance floor throwing shapes with King, Scarlett, and me. We all laugh and drink and have not a single care in the world.

"We've got each other," Scarlett says as we gather around in a little circle. "Our own little family."

"The music's stopped," King remarks.

"Yeah, it has."

I look back at the stage. The band is taking a little break.

I quickly disappear from the group. I see them all looking around for me. I head out the back to my car, where I've kept one final surprise.

My saxophone.

The one I haven't played for years. Not since that night Grace and I first slept together.

I sneak out onto the stage, reach the microphone, I sling the saxophone around my shoulder.

And I start playing the shining instrument.

Everyone at the wedding stops. Camilla looks over at me with a cheeky expression. Father halts mid-sentence. King and Scarlett hold each other.

And Grace is clearly gob smacked.

It all comes flooding back to me. I know how to play this thing. Grace rushes up to the stage, grinning from ear to ear.

"No way," she says. "I thought you said you stopped playing?"

I lean down to the microphone and take the instrument out of my mouth.

"I'm back now, Grace. I can play it again. And I dedicate this song to you."

She shakes her head at me in disbelief, but she better believe it.

This woman has changed me. For the better. I glance up at my brother and his wife. I wink. They wink back at me.

Our own little family.

How bloody true that statement is.

I can't wait to see what the future holds. Us four in this beautiful city we call home.

I look down from the stage at my wife.

She's the most beautiful thing in the entire world.

And from that dazzling gleam in her eyes, I know she's all mine.

Well, I'm all hers.

And then, for the first time in four years, I play my sax. For Grace.

ABOUT THE AUTHOR

Rebecca has had the storytelling bug since... forever!

What Rebecca likes most is writing steamy hot filthy romances with sweet happy endings sprinkled with some delicious bad boys.

Born and raised in an Aussie coastal town, she loves travelling around the world - meeting new people and discovering their stories.

Aside from adventuring she also enjoys a good rainy day in with a good book or at a hot beach catching the sun.

She's a world-class napping professional. You'll most likely find her asleep snuggled up on a sofa somewhere cozy.

For other titles and information please visit
rebeccacastle.com

facebook.com/rebeccacastleauthor
instagram.com/rebeccacastle.author

Printed in Great Britain
by Amazon